Also available by Douglas Hill

DEMON STALKERS: PREY
DEMON STALKERS: TORMENT

DEMON STALKERS

VENGEANCE

Douglas Hill

MACMILLAN CHILDREN'S BOOKS

First published 2009 by Macmillan Children's Books
a division of Macmillan Publishers Limited
20 New Wharf Road, London N1 9RR
Basingstoke and Oxford
Associated companies throughout the world
www.panmacmillan.com

ISBN 978-0-330-45219-9

1 3 5 7 9 8 6 4 2

A CIP catalogue record for this book is available from
the British Library.

Typeset by Intype Libra Limited
Printed in the UK by CPI Mackays, Chatham ME5 8TD

To the readers

1

It wasn't much of a track. Probably because no one had been brave enough to walk along it for a good while. Often it faded away almost to nothing, lost in the moor's coarse grass. And the heavy clouds and thin drizzle didn't make it any easier to see, especially with the afternoon light starting to fade.

I felt uneasy, but then uneasiness – with worry and alarm and fear and the rest of that gang – had been with me for a long time. Especially over the last two weeks or so. I'd pretty much learned to live with them.

Besides, my companion was striding on ahead, swinging her sturdy hiker's staff, as if the track was a paved road and as if she had never heard the word 'tired'. So I tramped steadily along behind her.

We didn't talk as we walked, which had become normal. We each tended to be lost in our own dark thoughts, as well as keeping a watchful lookout around us. But then Julia and I had never had much to say to each other.

She was the partner of a man who'd been a real friend of mine – a good man – and someone who was now lost . . . perhaps dead. Along with two others, also close friends – the only ones I'd ever had. So Julia and I had been thrown together, two sad survivors. I hadn't known her well before – and now it felt as if I'd never known her at all.

She looked the same, still thin, pale, faded-blonde Julia. But all her nervous, edgy timidity had simply vanished, as if she had thrown it off like an old coat.

The new Julia had a steely glint in her blue eyes and a determined set to her chin.

This Julia was fearless, and *tough*.

So clearly there'd always been more to her and, to my shame, I hadn't noticed.

Hadn't bothered to look.

But I was paying close attention to the new Julia. Without her I would have been lost and desolate, ready to do something totally insane and get myself killed. With her I had a purpose, a reason to stay alive as long as I could.

She had brought us from the city to that bleak wet moor, where she was looking for someone: a powerful person who might tell us how to find someone even more powerful, who might in turn help us locate the place that was our real goal – a place of unimaginable dangers.

And if all that wasn't enough, Julia and I both knew, as we walked on, that somewhere nearby something terrifying was looking for us.

That morning, when the sun was still pushing late-spring warmth through the massing clouds, we'd been in a small, cosy village talking to a small, cosy woman.

She was in charge of the post office, and Julia had gone to her to ask directions to an even smaller village.

'But we're not driving,' Julia had explained. 'We came here by coach.'

'Ooh,' the small woman said. 'On holiday, are you? You and your son?'

I'd been taken for Julia's son before, since we set out together, despite her lank blonde hair and my thick black hair. At other times, because I have the sort of lean, chiselled face that can look older than it is, people who weren't looking too closely had thought I was her boyfriend.

In fact, Julia was somewhere in her mid-thirties and I was only fourteen.

But then . . . I'd been fourteen for *years*.

'Yeah, that's right . . .' Julia said vaguely, '. . . a holiday.'

The small woman frowned, not sure what to make of us. We were both in worn shirts and jeans, with scruffy backpacks, travelling by coach . . . Not normal tourists.

'There's no bus to where you want to go,' she said at last. 'And it's a terrible long way round by road. Miles and miles.'

'Isn't there a shorter way over the moor?' Julia asked. 'Some kind of path?'

I twitched. Not long before, my four friends and I, including Julia, had spent some time on an otherworldly 'Path' – a path of untold horrors. And I didn't care for the word now.

The small woman shook her head. 'It's not a good path. And you don't want to be on the moor if the weather closes in.'

'Can you tell us where the path is?' Julia asked, ignoring the woman's concerns.

The small woman looked distinctly worried. 'I don't know, dear. No one ever walks that way now. There's . . . um . . . it can be dangerous . . .'

'Dangerous how?' Julia asked.

'It's hard to say.' The woman twisted her hands. 'Strange things . . .'

'Like what?' Julia said in a no-nonsense tone.

Hearing the edge in her voice, the small woman clearly decided not to argue any further – if we wanted to face bad weather and 'strange things' on the moor, it was our business. She wasn't going to make herself look even more silly and superstitious by trying to stop us. So from her doorway she pointed us to the gate that would take us on to the footpath, winding across a field and out into the small sea of grass and scrub brush.

We'd been walking for only ten minutes when the first spits of drizzle began.

We'd been walking for only half an hour when we heard the howling.

Julia didn't stop, just took a firmer grip on her staff and looked carefully at the empty moorland all around us. And I looked as well – while reaching for the knife sheathed at my hip. The always-sharp, unbreakable knife that only magical people could see.

The blade glowed bright silver, but I'd expected that. It turns golden when evil magic is nearby, but the howling had sounded fairly far away.

'Strange things . . .' I muttered. 'A farmer's dog? Or something hunting?'

'We haven't been hunted so far,' Julia said. 'It might be a sort of warning.' She went on, without further explanation, so I shrugged and followed. There was no point wasting energy worrying. Whatever had done the howling would probably show itself soon enough.

But as time passed and the drizzle faded and we kept walking along the barely visible path, we heard no more howls and saw nothing but wet grass and bushes.

Until at last, in that dim late afternoon, the path – getting more and more hard to see – wound along the foot of a slight incline with a dense cluster of thorny bushes and small twisted trees at the top of the slope. And Julia stopped.

'Up there,' she murmured. 'I'm sure that's it.'

I stared up the slope. I saw no house there, not even a hut. Wondering if the someone that Julia was looking for was a wild man who lived in thickets, I glumly followed as she set off up the incline. At the same time I drew the knife again, glad to see that the blade was still silvery.

But for no real reason – perhaps a nudge of instinct or intuition – I kept it ready in my hand, just in case.

And just as well.

We were only a few strides from the edge of the thicket when the greenery just ahead of us rustled violently.

And from it burst two dark beasts like huge growling dogs, but with the thick fur, slanted green eyes and glittering fangs of giant wolves.

2

I drifted to my left, trying to draw both of them away from Julia. But they smoothly separated and leaped at us. I had a glimpse of Julia swinging her staff but then going down under the weight of the wolf. In the same instant I slashed at the one attacking me, making it swerve away.

Then I turned and dived at the one snarling at Julia's throat.

Somehow, flat on her back on the grass, she was using her stout stick to block its jaws. I drove the knife at its neck, but it twisted away so that the blade left only a shallow gash, and in that moment the second wolf landed on my back.

I gasped as its fangs sank into my shoulder, tearing at the flesh. But I managed to hang on to the knife, stabbing blindly behind me, hearing the yelp as the blade went home. At the same time Julia, still on the ground, crashed the staff into the face of the other wolf, producing a second yelp.

And then a man's voice spoke a sharp word in a language I couldn't understand but had often heard. And the wolves were pulled away as if by invisible elastic cords.

As the man's dark shape loomed out of the thicket, and Julia got panting to her feet, leaning on her staff, I glanced at the knife again to confirm the amazing fact.

The blade was smeared and dripping with wolf-blood. But, beneath that redness, it glowed its normal silver.

The man seemed fairly young, in his twenties perhaps, wearing a black raincoat, dark trousers and shiny boots. He had a pale, strong-boned face, thick, dark shoulder-length hair and eyes the colour of the rain. And though he had called his wolves off, his glower didn't look friendly.

I'd seen his eyes widen slightly at the sight of the knife, so I knew he was magical.

Then he proved it, moving a hand above each of his wolves, making the wounds I'd given them disappear.

'What do you want here?' he snapped. 'This is private property.'

'Put up a sign,' I growled.

'You must be very anxious to stay hidden,' Julia said. 'With such sentries.'

The man's glower darkened even more. 'They

wouldn't have attacked if you had fled, as most intruders do. Most Powerless ones anyway, as I know you two are . . .'

He stopped, his eyes widening again, as he noticed that the gory damage to my shoulder was quietly repairing itself, as always.

Julia gave him a thin smile. 'I believe you're Ethan Wells, and we need to talk to you. My name's Julia McBride, and I live with someone you know, Paddy Gorman. And this –' she indicated me – 'is Nick Walker.'

The man, Ethan, nodded jerkily. 'Even here I've heard of the Changeless Boy. And of course I know Paddy. I suppose he must have told you about my place. But I still want to know what you're doing here.'

'We're here,' Julia said, 'to ask you to help us find your old teacher, Paddy's uncle Alderon—'

'No chance,' Ethan broke in harshly.

'*Because*,' Julia went on, her voice steely, 'Paddy has been *taken*, along with two others who are also close to us. And Alderon is the only mage I know of who might be able to help us, and help them.'

Ethan stared at her for a moment, his pale eyes glinting. 'Come in then, and tell me about it. But I promise nothing.' He turned to the wolves, who had never taken their eyes off us. 'Watch with care. If anything comes that is not human, kill it.'

*

It wouldn't have been fun pushing through the thicket's wet thorn-bushes, but the branches all helpfully swayed aside as we followed Ethan through them. In the heart of the thicket we came to the thick trunk of a big, old, half-dead tree – and I jumped when it suddenly turned into a tall, narrow door. Just a door, standing there with nothing but brush on either side.

But when it opened, it showed us a flight of polished steps, leading down. And when we went down, we found ourselves in a small, elegant underground house.

Nice hideaway, I thought. Magically secret, guarded by giant wolves, with Ethan's powers – fairly high-level, I thought – doing the housework and providing all the comforts. He even had a huge plasma TV.

But a hideaway meant that he was hiding *from* something. And I could guess what that might be. I also guessed that he was there on his own. He had that look – of someone who'd learned that loneliness is one of the prices you pay for safety. Along with non-stop, nerve-twisting watchfulness.

I'd learned that too, years before.

We settled in a cosy lounge with a warm fire burning without fuel. Ethan did us the favour of drying us off, magically, and mending my torn shirt. And I had a small lump in my throat, thinking of how often someone else had repaired me that way.

'Now tell me what's happened,' he said at last, as we

sipped cups of hot tea that had appeared from nowhere, 'and why you're seeking Alderon.'

Julia took a deep breath and began. But of course she started with the terrible, evil, violent happenings back in the late autumn and early winter.

For me, though, the story had its real beginnings years before – not long after I had actually turned fourteen.

At the time I'd been a street kid for a few years, alone and homeless ever since my mum finally drank herself to death. One night, looking for a place to sleep, I met a strange woman named Manta, all huge green eyes and red-gold hair. And I learned, the hard way, that magic was very real, and often horrifyingly evil.

Manta herself wasn't evil – she used her magic for good. Evil magic was mostly found in a group of power-hungry sorcerers called the Cartel.

Years before, they had stolen Manta's baby daughter – and, ever since, Manta had fought them and damaged them however she could.

So the Cartel had relentlessly hunted for her, aiming to kill her. And on the night I met her, one of their hunter-killers found her.

Despite her powers, Manta was forbidden to spill blood. So she made her escape – by pitting *me* against the Cartel's monster.

To help me, she gave me the magical knife. But more than that, Manta used a secret and powerful spell to make me changeless.

Since then I've been exactly the same – not ageing, not growing, not ever falling ill, never having to cut my hair or nails. Even if I was seriously hurt, I was always soon restored, with no scars or after-effects.

Still, I could be killed, in all sorts of ways, as long as they were quick. And that night I nearly was, until luck and desperation and the knife helped me kill the Cartel hunter and save my own skin.

But from then on the Cartel sent demon stalkers after me. And I managed to deal with them all. Still with luck and desperation but also with some survival-skills experience hard won along the way.

And then, less than a year before Julia and I walked out on to that moor, my life changed again in nearly every way.

3

The first step in that change was the truly amazing bit of luck when I met Paddy. He had a fair share of the *psychic* magic, mental powers like ESP, and he apparently decided that I needed help. So he took me home, and he and Julia made me feel part of a family for the first time in my lonely life.

Then that family got bigger, when we found April.

She was another lost kid, just fourteen, living rough – she was magical too, with a high level of the mental powers including ESP and psychokinesis (PK: moving things with the mind).

But she couldn't use them properly. She had a strange barrier in her mind that was blocking her powers and, stranger still, she had a *second* mental barrier blocking her memory. She could remember the previous few months, but almost nothing before that except her first name and a few disjointed images.

Paddy tried to help her with her powers, and the four of us felt like a family together. But I was still being stalked and eventually the Cartel captured me – and captured April as well.

In fact she had been their prisoner before – as a small child. They had known she was unusually high-powered and they wanted to make her serve them. So she and I were tortured – until pain and terror and sheer *fury* shattered one of the blockages in April's mind.

We were able to escape. But we paid a heavy price. Paddy and Julia were taken – sent to a terrible realm outside this reality. A Cartel private hell called the Downward Path. A place of swirling mists, where ghosts and demons lurked.

It took an old friend of Paddy's, Sam, to help us track them down, and finally we had to enlist the help of a creepy mage called Bertrand to secure our escape. But just when we thought the worst was behind us we had to face the most terrifying challenge of all – a confrontation with the great Head. And face it we did, but once again at what cost? Our loved ones were taken from us but we had no idea where to, and we were forced to enlist the reluctant help of others if we had any chance of finding them and getting them back alive. And the first step of our search had brought us to that hidden house on the rainswept moor.

*

Ethan sat without moving while Julia told our story, with a few additions from me. His face paled.

'If you fought the Cartel and escaped,' he said, his voice shaking, 'they must be searching for you! You could have led them *here*!'

'We've seen no signs of any hunters,' I said. 'And believe me – I'd know.'

'They think we're dead,' Julia added.

'It's a miracle that you're not,' Ethan said, looking less anxious. 'But Paddy and your other friends . . .'

'They're alive too,' Julia said sharply. 'I'm sure of it – and I'll go on believing it until I'm proved wrong. So I want to try to find them.'

'*We*,' I muttered. '*We* want to.'

She gave me a quick, grim smile, which became a scowl as she saw Ethan shaking his head.

'And that's why you want to find Alderon?' he said. 'To ask his help?'

Julia nodded. 'Paddy always said that his uncle Alderon is perhaps the most powerful mage in the country, the equal of the top level of the Cartel. And he told me once that Alderon has been magically studying the Cartel for many years, learning their secrets, on the principle of *know your enemy*. So we want him to help us find where our loved ones are – and to go there with us to rescue them.'

4

Ethan was still shaking his head. 'I'm fairly sure that Alderon wouldn't be able to help you. But I know for certain that I can't help you. I simply don't know where he is.'

Julia's face flushed. 'But you mu—'

'Alderon is very old now,' Ethan cut in with a sigh. 'And a few months ago, while he was spying on the Cartel, one of his veiling protections failed. So the Cartel discovered his intrusion.' He sighed again. 'I *warned* him endlessly. The Cartel is a danger to *all* independent higher-level mages, which is why I have lived here, in hiding, for so long. Alderon was taking *absurd* risks—'

'What happened?' Julia broke in sharply.

'Alderon finally went into hiding as well,' he said, 'cutting off all contact with friends and family to avoid endangering them. I've heard nothing from him since. I don't even know if he's still alive.'

Julia seemed to droop, her hope shattered, and

maybe I did too. 'Do *you* know where the Cartel headquarters is?' I asked.

'I haven't a clue,' Ethan said, 'and I don't want one. Anyway, you couldn't go there on your own, the two of you. They'd kill you.'

That was so obvious it didn't need a comment, but somehow it made Julia and me straighten up again. 'Can you think of anyone who *might* help us?' she asked.

'Not really . . .' He paused, peering at the indelible Mark of Changelessness on my throat. 'I heard that you were made changeless by a secret spell known only to that witch . . . Manda?'

'Manta,' I said.

He nodded. 'And she's apparently been fighting the Cartel for years. So she might know, and might even be willing to go with you . . .'

'No,' I said. 'I only ever saw her that once. She sent me a lot of vague dream-messages, after, but even those have stopped. The Cartel was furiously hunting her, and I think they got her.'

'She might also be hiding,' Ethan said. 'Which would be sensible.'

'Either way, she's no use to us,' I said. And nothing new there, I thought.

'What will you do, then?' he asked.

'We'll keep looking,' Julia said. 'Wherever and

however we can. So – could you tell us at least where Alderon was living before he went into hiding? We might find some clue there, to where he's gone.'

'I doubt that,' Ethan said. 'He'd expect the Cartel to be looking.'

'We'd look from a different viewpoint,' Julia said, her voice steely again.

So Ethan gave in and told us the name of the village where the old mage had lived, and which house it had been.

He also begged us to take great care, and not to make ourselves too visible when we went to look around that place. And because by then twilight would be gathering outside, Ethan also decided that it wouldn't be a good idea for us to leave – though he seemed less worried about us getting lost on the moor than about us straggling into a village in the middle of nowhere, late at night, looking for a place to stay, and making people wonder where we'd been.

So, a bit grudgingly, he gave us a fairly sparse and tasteless dinner, eaten mostly in wary silence, and put us up for the night. Julia got a spare room, I got the sofa in the lounge. And, as usual, I took a long while getting to sleep, struggling to keep from thinking about what might be happening to April and Sam and Paddy, if they were still alive.

Such thoughts were always painful and did me no good at all.

So I thought about magic and mages for a while. I wondered if fearful Ethan really thought his underground house and his wolves would save him if the Cartel came after him. I wondered about mysterious Alderon – if he was alive, if we could find him, if he was too old and feeble and frightened to be any use to anyone.

I even thought about bony Bertrand, the mage in skeleton form who had betrayed us to the Cartel when we got back to this world, hoping to get his body back.

And that got me thinking about his ex-wife – Manta.

But I wasn't thinking about their marriage. And I didn't let myself think about my firm belief that April was Manta's daughter, stolen from her by the Cartel. That hardly mattered, when it was all too likely that I'd never see April again . . .

No, I was thinking about Manta's powers, and her courage, and the battles she had fought against the Cartel for so long. There had been a time when I'd hated her for making me changeless, and so putting the demon stalkers on my trail. But I'd mostly got over that.

Right then I was thinking what an ally Manta would be, for Julia and me.

But I told myself to forget it. If she was alive at all, she was probably better hidden than poor Ethan in his bunker or ancient Alderon wherever he was.

So we'll find no help anywhere, I thought bitterly. Everyone's in hiding, trying to save their skins.

Everyone but Julia and me.

When I finally did fall into a restless sleep, I had one of my ugliest dreams ever. I could have done with one of Manta's helpful dream-messages, but instead it was a major nightmare.

In a vast room so high I couldn't see the ceiling, the monstrous Head of the Cartel rested on a high platform of gleaming stone. It was as terrifying as when I'd first seen it for real, with its deathly grey skin, its tangled white hair and beard, its slitted crimson eyes. And though it was silent, its mouth was open wide – showing evilly pointed teeth and a depth of darkness from which its breath came in gusts that stank like rotting flesh.

And April was on that platform – barefoot in a plain white dress, her long brown hair limp and dull, her big hazel eyes blank and empty.

In my sleep I thrashed and groaned. In my dream I watched in helpless horror as April walked calmly up to the monstrosity's gaping mouth – and stepped inside.

And as the terrible mouth closed on her, I came

awake with a choked yell. No one seemed to hear it, but I didn't care if they had.

Lying there shivering and sweating, I had a ghastly feeling that it might have been a nightmare with a meaning. Perhaps it was simply telling me what I didn't want to accept – that April was no longer alive.

Or perhaps it was saying something that would in fact be *worse*. That April had at last been broken, and corrupted – and her powers enslaved by the Cartel.

5

In the very early morning, breakfast was as sparse as dinner had been and took less time. Ethan clearly wanted to get rid of us as much as we wanted to get going. And he took us the back way out of his hidden home, along a narrow, dank tunnel and up through a disguised trapdoor.

'I'd wish you luck,' he said, looking gloomy, 'but you need more than that. I just hope you'll come to see that this *quest* of yours is pointless and hopeless, and almost certainly will get you killed.'

That less than cheery farewell, which didn't tell us anything we didn't know, sent us on our way. Back on the moor, weak sunlight was glinting on the damp grass, and the knife glinted silvery. And we saw no other living being, not even a sheep, all the way to the little village we'd asked directions to the previous day.

Ethan had told us that old Alderon's former home was in a small village not all that far away. And Julia had taken a surprising amount of cash out of the bank before we left the city, so we were able to go there the easy way. Another post-office lady put us on to a grumpy yokel who ran a part-time taxi service, since there was only one bus a week. And off we went.

It was a silent trip, since the driver was no more chatty than we were. I stared out at wet fields and hedgerows, trying to block the memory of my nightmare. And Julia stared blankly straight ahead, maybe struggling with nightmares of her own.

When we got to the village we let the taxi go, then at once regretted it. The place looked mostly deserted. The tall dark house that Alderon had lived in looked even worse, not just abandoned but vandalized, with broken windows and smashed doors. Peering through a window, we saw more signs of wreckage. And there was a whiff of scorched wood, as if someone had tried to torch the place, along with the stink of rising damp and cat spray.

'Maybe not vandals,' I muttered. 'Maybe some demon stalker trashed the place when he found the old man gone.'

Still, we went in and looked around fairly thoroughly. But when we found absolutely nothing except more damage and bad smells, we were glad to get out of the place.

And then we just stood in the silent, dusty street and looked at each other.

'What now?' I asked.

'I don't know,' Julia said, looking as unhappy as I felt. 'We could look around the village, talk to some of the people . . . See if anyone knows anything.'

'See if anyone's *alive*,' I muttered.

In fact, more and more, the whole place seemed dead. Most of the houses were unoccupied, some boarded up, all sagging into ruin. And in the few places that did look lived-in we saw no sign of movement or activity. Nor was anyone out on the crumbling pavements, as we wandered along, except a prowling grey cat that was probably responsible for some of the stink at Alderon's house.

The cat walked along with us for a bit, as if glad of the company. But then it turned away and slipped through a partly open door in a run-down cottage. When we spotted a few signs in one window, hinting that it might be some sort of shop, we peered through the door and then went in.

The front room of the cottage offered a plain wooden counter and a lot of cluttered, dusty shelves holding mostly tinned food. Between counter and shelves stood a thin, stooped old woman in a long heavy dress with a stained apron, blinking at us with surprise.

'Goodness!' she said, in a thin quavery voice like a bird's twitter. 'Where did you come from? Are you lost?'

Julia smiled, and gently explained why we were there.

'Oh, dear, no,' the old lady twittered. 'Old Mr Gorman, Alderon, moved away some time ago. Never said where he was going.' A sigh rattled in her throat. 'Near everyone's moved away. All the young folk left years ago, no work for them here . . . Just a few of us old ones left now, waiting . . . for the end.'

That was sad – and for us even sadder when a few more questions produced not the tiniest scrap of information. But she did tell us that there was a small town with a pub not too many miles down the road, where we could eat and find rooms if we wanted.

It was better than nothing, but only just. And as we set off, I didn't even bother asking 'What now?' again. I knew the crushing, despairing answer.

We'd reached a dead end. Alderon was gone – maybe even dead. Neither Julia nor I knew anyone else to ask, anywhere else to look. In the midst of the ruined village, our small feeble hopes of helping our loved ones had also collapsed in ruins.

With nothing else to do, we started trudging gloomily along the narrow country road towards the town that the old lady had mentioned. The late morning had got overcast again, which suited our mood. All we need now, I thought sourly, is to get drenched by more rain.

But it stayed more or less dry as we walked on, eventually coming to an old country church by the roadside. It was one of those small plain ones, all dark stone with what looked like a low square tower instead of a spire. And it had a fairly big churchyard full of gravestones, some looking ancient. I thought of the old lady, and the other old villagers, waiting to fill more places in that churchyard as their empty lives faded away . . .

Then I twitched, reaching for the knife.

In my years on the streets, and more years being hunted, I'd got good at the most important survival skill of all. Being on guard. No matter how deep I was in misery or happiness or any other thoughts or feelings, I never stopped being watchful.

So I'd caught a glimpse, on the edge of my vision, of a flash of movement in the grass and weeds on the fringe of the churchyard.

'What is it?' Julia asked.

'I saw something,' I muttered.

But the knife was still silvery, nothing horrible burst out of the long grass and I suddenly realized what it was I'd glimpsed.

'It's all right,' I said, putting the knife away. 'I think it was just that grey cat from the village.'

Julia's head came up as she stared intently around. 'The cat? The one that followed us before?' Now staring even more intently at the church's square tower, she turned off the road, on to the gravelly path leading to the church.

'What are you doing?' I asked.

'Looking,' she said. 'For someone who is, or was, one of the greatest mages in the land. And for a cat that followed us before, and is still following us.'

It wasn't hard to work out. 'You think the cat belongs to Alderon?'

'Possibly,' she said. 'And if it has followed us here, out of the village, it could mean that . . . Alderon is here. In that church.'

If so, I thought, it would be a clever hiding place. If he left his house in apparent fright and went into hiding, no one would expect he'd just go down the road a little way. So we might as well have a look in the church.

But there was no way in. The church looked as abandoned as the village, with thick wooden doors solidly locked and metal-mesh screens protecting its windows. No way in, even for the cat, which had disappeared.

I saw Julia looking up at the little tower, and I looked too. It had some of those ugly carvings, 'gargoyles', that were made in olden times as waterspouts from the guttering on church roofs. Like many that I'd seen, these gargoyles – one at each corner of the tower – had devil faces and bat wings. Probably the old builders' idea of a joke, to annoy the pious.

In that moment Julia gasped and I flinched – as a powerful unseen force from nowhere took hold of us. Hoisting us into the air, it flattened us against the damp stone wall near the top of the tower and held us there.

And on the nearest corner of the tower, a weathered stone gargoyle turned its head to look at us, spread its bat wings and bared long fangs.

6

I felt as cold as the wall we were pressed against. Our time of safety had clearly come to an end, as I'd known it would. The Cartel had discovered us, and this stony horror was what they had sent to kill us.

We couldn't even see it properly, since it was on the wall to one side, on our right. And we couldn't move our eyes or anything else. Julia's face was stark white as she struggled, uselessly, against the unseen power that held us. But I just watched, from the corner of my eye, looking for the tiniest chance to break free and fight.

The gargoyle growled, sounding like stone scraping stone. 'Clearly you are not just idle tourists,' it rasped, 'nor dull scholars inspecting an old church. Yet I can sense that you are both Powerless – which may be an excellent disguise and is certainly a mystery. Why are you creeping around here?'

'Who wants to know?' I snarled.

The gargoyle growled again. 'I am one who could

lock you in this church's crypt for a week or so, in the dark with the dead, till you respond properly.'

That stopped me for a moment, and Julia took over. 'We're looking for an elderly gentleman named Alderon,' she said stiffly, 'who is the uncle of my partner, Paddy Gorman. And since you don't look like him, I imagine he is speaking through you.'

The creature lowered its wings, looking as surprised as its stony devil-face could manage. 'So you would be Julia,' it grated. 'Yes – I see it is so. And this scowling youth . . .'

It craned forward so it could see all of us, especially my left side. Where the knife was sheathed.

'Of course,' it growled. 'The Changeless Boy. I heard that my nephew had taken you in.'

Suddenly, with no sense of movement, Julia and I were standing on a carpet in a large and cluttered room that was warm and airy, though I could see no heating and no windows. In a low cushiony armchair in front of us sat a very old man, totally hairless, as wrinkled as a forgotten apple, with a light blanket over his legs and one thin hand on a heavy stick of unpolished wood.

And Julia and I were still held motionless in the grip of his power.

'Now explain yourselves,' he said, his voice almost as

stony as the gargoyle's. 'Most especially, tell me how you came to be in this place.'

'We visited Ethan,' Julia began, and told him briefly how we had got to that village and that church.

'And you spotted the cat, who watches strangers on my behalf,' muttered the old man, who was obviously Alderon. 'Very sharp-eyed of you.' His face creased even more as he glowered. 'But don't assume that I have become helpless in old age. I sense no powers in you and no threat from you – but if that *is* just a disguise, and you have been sent by the Cartel, I will kill you before you can begin an attack.'

'We haven't been,' I snarled. 'And you're the only one doing any attacking.'

'In fact,' Julia added, just as sharply, 'we want your help *against* the Cartel.'

Alderon snorted. 'That is either a poor joke or a weak-minded fantasy.'

I saw anger ignite in Julia's eyes. 'Listen, old man. Your nephew is a prisoner of the Cartel, along with two others whom we care about a great deal. So we need your help, to help them – unless your powers have faded into nothing but an arrogant manner and a few tired tricks.'

Alderon's sunken old eyes filled with rage as well. He half raised his stick, and the room was suddenly vibrating with power, as if a giant invisible dynamo had just started up.

But then he slowly lowered the stick again, his anger faded and the small rasping sound he made might have been a sigh.

And in the same instant the magic that held us still vanished, freeing us.

'Through that outburst I can sense that you are truly what you say you are,' he said. 'And I can see why Paddy was drawn to you. I wish I had met you in less troubled times . . .'

'You might have,' Julia snapped, 'if you'd ever been in touch with Paddy.'

'Indeed,' Alderon murmured. 'But we were never close, he and I, and there was never an occasion . . . I was engaged in many important matters, including the instruction of leading young mages . . .'

'And Paddy was only a middle-level psychic,' Julia said, her voice tight. 'Not *important* enough.'

The old man sighed again. 'No doubt that too will seem like *arrogance* on my part, and perhaps it is so. But despite all that, I'm truly sorry to hear of my nephew's plight. Will you tell me how it happened?'

So Julia and I told him our story as we had told Ethan. And the old mage sat without moving or blinking, taking it all in.

'If someone else had related all that to me,' he said

at last, 'I would have thought it quite impossible for you to have lived through it.' He peered at me. 'It seems, my boy, that people should start calling you the Changeless *Warrior*. Indeed, both of you have shown quite remarkable qualities . . .'

'Not remarkable enough,' I muttered.

'That is regrettably, undeniably, so,' Alderon said. 'But *no one* has the qualities or the powers to oppose the Cartel. You have seen its grotesque Head and glimpsed his monstrous power. Even alone, he is many times mightier than the greatest mage who ever lived – beyond me even in my prime. And his power is reinforced by the notable sorcerers who serve him. So, you see, the harsh fact is that I cannot help you or your loved ones. Indeed, they must surely already be beyond any help.'

'They're not dead!' Julia burst out. 'I *know* they're not!'

Alderon tilted his head, peering at her. 'You may well be right, but that is beside the point. They are as much out of your or anyone's reach as if they *were* dead. If Paddy and Sam Foss still live, they are probably being tormented and abused in many vile ways. And as for the girl . . .'

'Her name is April,' I said.

'Of course.' He nodded. 'If *April* is who I think she is, I know something of why they have pursued her so endlessly. And they will certainly keep her alive, to fulfil what they see as her destiny. Which is nothing less than to strengthen and enhance the Cartel, to alter it from merely an evil but limited group into a monstrous force capable of ruling, or destroying, the world.'

7

His words horrified me, but they flung Julia into a fury. 'April would *die* before she'd let herself be a part of that!'

Alderon nodded sadly. 'In brutal truth, it would be preferable if she did. But they will not let her die, and she will not be able to resist. They will find a way to corrupt her or enslave her, and she will do their bidding.'

'You can't *know* that,' I said.

'In fact I can,' the old man said. 'As Ethan told you, I have been studying the Cartel for many years, watching them by means of ESP and various spells. I was never foolish enough to risk spying on the Head, though I have glimpsed him when he emerged from the secret base where he lives. But through watching and listening to the leading sorcerers, I came to hear of a well-kept secret that even they spoke of only in cryptic whispers. A secret concerning a *prophecy*.'

'About April?' I asked.

'About a girl child,' Alderon said. 'Nearly twenty years ago, one of the Cartel's greatest psychics and seers delivered the prophecy. It was about a girl whom he called the Empowered Child. A girl to be born of a mage and a powerful witch . . .'

That made me jump, but I said nothing.

'. . . who even in childhood would be far more powerful than her parents,' Alderon went on. 'And who would develop into the greatest, the mightiest mage the world has ever known. Gifted with both psychic powers and the higher magic on a level of power never known before.' He peered at us sadly. 'And your April must be that Child, since the Cartel have pursued her so avidly.'

'And they want her great power to serve them,' Julia whispered.

'Indeed,' Alderon said. 'And to make them supreme, when she is fully grown and her magic fully developed. But unfortunately . . .' he shook his bald head, 'in all my watching I never learned exactly what it was she would *do*, when grown up, to serve that purpose.'

'She'd commit evil,' I muttered. 'It's what the Cartel does.'

'No!' Julia cried. 'She *won't*! We have to find her, save her . . . Alderon, in the face of that appalling threat, you *must* help us!'

The old man seemed to shrink slightly in his chair.

'My dear,' he said softly, 'if I *could* help you, trying to do so would merely hasten my death and yours . . .'

'I don't *care*!' Julia groaned.

'But the fact is,' Alderon said, holding up a shaky hand, 'I *cannot* help you. I'm not doing all that well helping myself.' He sighed again. 'Ethan told you that I was discovered. I was spying on a top-level Cartel sorcerer named Doul, and . . . he sensed my gaze. Perhaps I had grown careless, in old age. Certainly I had grown slower – so before I could break away, Doul's magic backtracked my ESP and located me. And, even worse, he hurled a spell at me along that track.'

'Ethan didn't mention that,' I said.

'He didn't need to know,' Alderon said. 'The spell is a magical *infection*, which slowly devours my flesh. I was able to resist it, magically, even as I fled from my home and hid myself here behind a battery of veiling magics. But I can never rid myself totally of the infection. Each time I fight it off, thinking I'm cured, it returns. And each time I find it harder to fight than before.' His wrinkles shifted as he grimaced. 'I cannot say how much time I have left. But before too long, I know, it will be too strong for me.'

Julia's jaw clenched. 'That's sad, and I'm sorry for you. But think, Alderon. If you're dying anyway, from a Cartel evil, why not strike back at them by helping us?'

'It would of course be a noble way to go,' the old man said. 'But it's beyond me. I'm old and tired and the damage from the infection has left me infirm, confined to this chair. I could only travel magically. But the moment I left my protections here, the Cartel would know – and would then discover you as well, if we were together. They would erase us before we got fully started. Even if I tried to strike at them from here, they could backtrack again and find me. Besides, the higher magic always has limitations over distance.'

I slumped, feeling crushed, seeing Julia's eyes fill with tears. Everything he'd said was true, no question. And it left us helpless, with no idea where to go and little hope of staying alive long enough to go anywhere.

'There must be *something* that can be done to help them,' Julia breathed.

'I wish there was,' Alderon said.

I straightened. 'There's one thing,' I snarled. 'You said something about the Cartel's "secret base". Tell us where it is.'

'Even if I knew,' Alderon murmured, 'I'm not sure I'd tell you. It would be like feeding you into the fire. But in fact I never discovered its location.'

'Not even a hint?' I asked.

His small laugh held no humour. 'Hints, yes. One or two strange mentions of a special secret place known only as "the island". And a suggestion that it may be off the east coast somewhere. But that means it's an island in the *sea*. Which could hardly be their headquarters.'

It couldn't be much use to them for anything, I thought sourly. Not even the most powerful spells could get magical people across salt water.

But Julia had also straightened up from her despondent droop, looking as if she'd thought of something. 'You mentioned a top Cartel sorcerer named Doul. What can you tell us about him?'

'The Cartel always has three highest-level sorcerers at the top,' Alderon said. 'Running the organization, in direct contact with the Head. Recently the top three were Redman, Kannis and Doul.' He smiled his wintry smile again. 'When the young warrior here helped to get rid of Redman, your friend Fray took his place. Now, with Fray gone, they haven't yet chosen a replacement. They may be finding it difficult.'

'Redman had a house in the country,' Julia said, still looking thoughtful. 'Do you know where Kannis and Doul live?'

The old man's frown deepened. 'I'm not sure about Kannis. He's the dominant one of the three, so it may be that he lives at the Cartel base, wherever it is. But Doul has a house in one of the eastern counties . . . And I do hope you're not thinking of going anywhere near it.'

There were no more tears in Julia's eyes. They had

regained their sapphire glint, and her jaw was set firm again. And I started to smile, because I knew exactly what she was thinking.

'We might go very near,' she said lightly. 'To see if we can find something or someone to tell us where we can find our loved ones.'

8

Alderon looked as if he wanted to argue with her, but the look in her eyes made him give it up. Instead he tried to ease the mood that had overtaken us by playing host. His magic produced a big dining table from somewhere, already heaped with good things to eat. Despite everything, the sight made my mouth water, and even Julia looked ready to eat. But as we moved to the table, I saw what Alderon had meant about being 'infirm'.

He moved with us without getting up, magically floating his chair to the table.

But as he moved, the light cover slipped part-way from his lap, and I glimpsed the shiny cloth wrapped around his lower legs. Which came to an end too soon, because he had no feet. Just bandaged stumps.

'As I said,' he sighed, seeing that we'd noticed, 'I'm struggling to keep the evil disease at bay, but . . . it's winning.' His voice trembled. 'Once, even twenty years ago, they would not have found it so easy to bring me down.'

I thought about that as Julia murmured with sympathy, and as we poked at our food, suddenly no longer hungry. 'Alderon,' I asked, 'if you really had that much power back then, didn't you ever think of *taking on* the Cartel? Maybe linking up with other high-level mages like Sam, maybe Ethan . . . You might have put an end to them years ago!'

The old man slowly shook his head. 'If it had just been a gathering of sorcerers, Kannis and so forth, I would certainly have rallied Sam Foss and my other prodigies against them. But not against the Cartel's monstrous leader. He is powerful beyond measure, beyond any group of mages.'

'Are you sure?' Julia asked. 'You said you've never dared to spy on him.'

Alderon's old eyes glinted as he peered at us. 'That's so, but I've heard about him from his minions. I believe that the gigantic Head is in fact a *guise* – worn by someone or something who is not human. He may in fact be a *high demon* from some terrible realm beyond our world, as magically powerful as he is evil. Trying to strike at him, even with other mages, would be like mice marching against a tiger.'

He clearly wasn't just explaining himself but warning us. But though Julia looked troubled, I managed a thin smile.

'Good image,' I said. 'But mice don't "*march*". They know how to creep around in shadows and hide in holes and survive – even in a tiger's den.'

That made Julia smile too, because she knew I was as determined as she was. And it was Alderon's turn to look troubled.

He still went on playing host though, and it seemed as if he was in no hurry to send us on our way. I thought he was trying by small kindnesses to make up for the fact that he couldn't – and anyway wouldn't – help us.

So he kept us there through that day, talking around the subject of the Cartel – telling stories of his great days as a mage, listening with interest to Julia talking fondly of her time with Paddy. Much later, after we'd nibbled at another huge spread of food, he offered us beds for the night – quite a bit more comfortable than Ethan's.

There I slept deeply without any kind of nightmares. Perhaps because the big grey cat came to curl up on the covers beside me, lulling me with its purr.

But in the morning Alderon troubled us again.

Julia and I managed to eat quite a lot of the huge breakfast that he gave us. And we were properly grateful when the old man offered us a fairly huge wad of cash to help us on our way. He had more than he needed, he told us. Then his eyes filled.

'Paddy would have inherited my money,' he murmured. 'But now . . . It will be unbearably sad if even with this disease I outlive my nephew – as I shall probably outlive you two, if you insist on taking up this impossible quest.'

And he was right – that was a sad thought. But that wasn't what really troubled us. It was what he said when Julia asked if his magic would take us out of the old church, his place of safety, as it had brought us in.

'Not exactly,' Alderon told her, looking uneasy.

That made me tense up. 'You don't have any idea,' I said, scowling, 'of *keeping* us here? So we don't betray you and your hideout to the Cartel?'

'I thought of that,' he admitted. 'But I know you would be unwilling guests, and I'm not in the habit of holding people against their will . . .'

'Good,' I said through my teeth.

'So, instead,' he went on, 'I've decided that when you leave I'll protect my secret another way. It's quite easy, and totally harmless, to change a person's memory . . .'

Julia turned pale and backed away. 'Stay out of our minds!' she cried.

'I would never think of invading your thoughts, or your inmost secrets,' Alderon said firmly. 'Your experience of this place is so recent that it is still uppermost in your memories, quite easy to deal with.'

'Deal with how?' I demanded.

'I will move you magically away from this place,' Alderon said, 'but you will be unaware of it. When you arrive where I will put you, you will still remember me and much of our time together. But you will remember *nothing* of where this place is, or where I am.'

'Can you do that?' Julia asked, frowning.

Alderon sighed. 'It is already done. Farewell to you both, my dears.'

As he spoke my eyes blurred, and as I closed them I saw Julia close hers. I felt a strange, soft whisper of a breeze around me, as if a window had been opened. Then I found myself sitting in a warm place, feeling the hum and sway of movement . . .

When I opened my eyes and stared around, Julia and I were sitting together in a back seat on a large coach, rolling through a totally different countryside.

9

I glanced around, but none of the other passengers were staring at us – as they would be if we'd just *appeared* in the coach. So, somehow, Alderon must have controlled them too.

'Stubborn old goat,' Julia said angrily.

She seemed frustrated at having got so little help from the old man. But I just shrugged. I understood Alderon wanting to keep himself hidden. Julia and I weren't exactly advertising ourselves. Staying hidden had to do with surviving – and I knew a lot about that.

'At least he's sent us in the right direction,' I told Julia. 'And don't forget – he could just as easily have kept us quiet a more *permanent* way.'

She blinked, thought about it, slowly nodded. 'I suppose you're right.'

'We just passed a road sign,' I said. 'We're nearly at the city.'

Where it would be easy to get another coach, that

would take us to another city. Smaller than the capital, but the largest centre in the eastern counties.

Where we might just find information showing us the whereabouts of a sorcerer named Doul.

So we travelled on, got off that coach, got on another, kept travelling. Before too long we were rolling along a pleasant highway through amazingly flat farmland under a wide blue sky, not far from that smaller eastern city. With the sun dipping down towards the horizon behind us, we'd find a place to stay overnight, and start looking for Doul in the morning.

But I knew it wouldn't be easy.

A library might have directories for the counties of that region, as well as for the city. But I didn't think Doul would be listed, with phone number and everything, as if he was an ordinary citizen.

And even if he lived in a big posh house, I didn't think he'd have got too chummy with the locals. Being an evil and murderous sorcerer didn't quite fit with playing country squire.

He might even be using a different name around there, which would make him even harder to find.

Or he might somehow become aware of us, as we searched for him. And then we'd find him – in a really unpleasant way. Bringing our journey to a sharp and grisly end.

But there's never any point twisting the nerves and draining the energies worrying about what might happen. I tend just to get on with the present and deal with the future as it comes.

So I wrenched my mind away from thoughts of possible failure and disaster, and made myself think instead about one of my favourite subjects. April.

Alderon had done me a great favour when he revealed the big Cartel prophecy about the Empowered Child. A lot of questions that had been biting at me were suddenly answered.

Now I knew that I was probably right about April being Manta's daughter. But, far more importantly, now I knew exactly why the Cartel had been so obsessed with capturing April and keeping her alive.

So there was every chance that she *was* still alive. And maybe, as always before, fighting with all her power to keep them from enslaving her.

A good reason to stay alive ourselves, I thought grimly. To help her.

The late-spring evening was still managing to be not quite dark when we got to the coach station in the city. A group of local lads were hanging around, making a lot of noise, glowering at the arriving passengers. I ignored them, and Julia – who had been in one of her long silences – hardly noticed them.

Walking along the streets, I peered around into the

shadows as warily as I always did. But I saw only an assortment of ordinary people going along in their ordinary ways. And Julia didn't seem to see much at all – drawn into herself, a bit hunched and tense and nervy, the way she used to be.

'What is it?' I asked finally.

'Sorry,' she murmured. 'I'm sort of on edge. I keep thinking that Doul might not be far away. And he could have magical alarms set up, or something.'

'He could,' I said flatly. 'We might have been spotted already. It's hard to hide from mages, as we found with Ethan and Alderon. But it probably isn't that much harder here than anywhere else.'

She peered at me, then managed a bleak smile. 'You're a true fatalist, Nick. Such a comfort.'

I shrugged. 'I'm not sure I know what you mean. I think I'm just a realist. And here's some reality for you. I was told – by Redman himself – that when the Cartel was hunting me, they didn't always know where I was. Their watchers or whatever aren't one hundred per cent reliable. So maybe Doul's alarms aren't either.'

Her smile widened a little. 'Now that *is* comforting.'

Not too far from the station we spotted a little guest house offering the usual B&B. It was cheap enough and we saw no reason to look any further, and started for the door. But then I slowed and paused.

Along the darkening street I'd noticed two big lads,

probably in their late teens, wearing dark jeans and tight T-shirts that showed off their bulk. I was fairly sure they'd been part of the group at the station.

I was very sure that they were staring at us.

I nearly reached for the knife, but stopped. I didn't use the knife against ordinary people unless I really had to. And even if they were would-be muggers, we were only a few steps from the guest-house door. So I turned away, and we went in.

A cheery young woman gave us a room at the back of the house – twin beds and a cramped shower room. Julia and I had shared, without any problem, since we started out together. We were both fairly private people, and we'd worked out ways of managing without it being too awkward or embarrassing. I'd often shared with others in the same way, including April.

The important point was that Julia and I would be *together*, if something from the Cartel came for us in the night.

And of course we didn't take silly chances. It would have been nice to have a fresh breeze in the room, but we weren't going to leave our window open over an unlit back garden. And we usually took turns sleeping.

That night Julia took the first turn on watch, probably thinking troubled thoughts in the darkness. And after Alderon and everything, I fully expected another brutal nightmare.

Instead I slept fairly well until some time in the middle of the night. And then it wasn't a bad dream that jolted me awake.

I heard Julia's soft hiss at the same moment as I heard the quiet scrape of metal on metal, like a key turning a lock.

And I saw the line of faint light, from the hallway outside our room, as the door slowly began to open.

10

Neither Julia nor I moved a muscle as two hulking dark shapes moved slowly into the room. I'd already slid a hand under my pillow as the door opened, to grip the hilt of the knife. I had a feeling that this might be a time when I'd have to use it against Powerless people. But for that moment I lay still, waiting.

Then I flinched and Julia gasped as the ceiling light flashed on. And a rough voice with an eastern-counties accent growled at us, 'Stay quiet, both of you. You scream or make a move, you get this.'

Blinking in the light, I saw that the growler was holding up a wicked-looking combat knife, while the other held some kind of short heavy club. I also saw that they were the two louts I'd seen before, outside, watching us. They looked like brothers, both tall and beefy with round, stupid faces and dirty-brown hair.

Clearly they preferred to do their mugging in private, off the street. I wondered how they'd got the key to the room. But mostly I wondered what they'd do next.

Ignoring Julia, whom they obviously regarded as no kind of threat, the two of them moved warily to loom over the bed where I lay, watching and waiting.

'You still get a funny feelin' about this one?' asked the one with the club.

The knife-wielder shrugged. 'I get somethin'. He don't feel right, not natural.' He glowered at me. 'Maybe let's put him to sleep, take him to Headley. Might be somethin' that'd please the master, get us taken in.'

'Rob 'em first though,' the other one chortled. 'And maybe have a bit of fun with that skinny cow too . . .'

By then I was getting my own kind of funny feeling – about what they might be, aside from muggers. And weighing up who their 'master' might be.

And I was carefully gathering myself to come up off the bed at their throats when Julia got there first.

With a shriek of pure fury she exploded upward, landing on the back of the club-wielder. And before he could begin to move she had wrapped her legs around his middle and clamped an arm across his throat.

It was a classic hold, the hand of the choking arm braced by her other arm. But I wasn't waiting to admire it. As Julia's opponent gargled and toppled backwards on to her bed, with her underneath but still grimly clinging on, the startled knife-man began to swing around towards them.

I leaped just as Julia had, slashing at his forearm. And as he howled, dropping his knife and stumbling back, I realized two remarkable things. First, the knife's glow was silver, so these two weren't Cartel. Second, the thug's eyes had widened at the sight of the knife. Which meant, since he could see it, that he was magical.

But in the fraction of an instant that I noticed those things, I was also snatching up the three-legged bedside table and smashing it down on to the knife-man's head.

Whirling towards the other bed, I saw Julia pushing aside the limp body of the other one. Not dead – just unconscious from the choke-hold.

'You're stronger than you look,' I said with a half-grin.

She shrugged. 'Fear and fury will do that.'

'It takes nerve too,' I said. 'How did you get so *tough*?'

I'd asked the question lightly, but her gaze was serious. 'The same way you did, when you became changeless. From fighting back when you were attacked. From doing anything and everything to survive. From endless rage and hate aimed at whatever threatened that survival.'

I nodded silently. She was exactly right. That was the

fuel that had kept me going, and the fuel that was keeping us on our journey.

Luckily we both had an ample supply.

She prodded with a bare toe at one of the unconscious thugs. 'They'll be out for a while. And the police might keep them busy, if they're found here with the key to this room. I wonder how they got it?'

'They're low-level psychics,' I said.

Her startled look showed that she'd been too busy with her battle to hear what they had said to me.

'They probably used that power to get the key,' I went on. 'They had some kind of dim "feeling" about me, and they talked about putting me to sleep. To take me to their "master" – and maybe get "taken in" . . .'

Julia's eyes went wide. 'Into the Cartel! It must be! And the Cartel master in this region . . .'

'Almost definitely Mr Doul,' I said, smiling again because I'd saved the best for last. 'And they said *where* they'd take me. Some place called Headley – most likely a village around here, maybe fairly near.'

'A good place for a Cartel house,' Julia said wryly. 'I wonder if the Head ever visits Headley.' She turned away, suddenly brisk. 'Let's get out of here, as quietly as we can, and find it.'

Quickly she ripped up a sheet and tied the two sleepers hand and foot, with even a bandage on the arm of the one I'd cut. Then we dressed and crept downstairs, to find the guest-house owner asleep behind the small counter. Where the keys were kept.

Julia had paid for the room on arrival, but she left a bit extra to replace the ruined sheet. On the streets a few early birds and early workers were stirring as the eastern sky signalled the arrival of morning. We had breakfast in a cafe among some of those workers, and when the city was fully awake we went looking for a library.

By then we were a useful distance from the guest house, where someone would soon be finding the unexpected twosome in our room. In the library I expected a slow nerve-racking search through local directories, but Julia surprised me yet again.

On one of the computers offered for public use she swiftly went online and found what we were looking for in seconds.

Not a village, but a house. *In* a village, only a few miles away. A big old manor house called Headley Hall.

Where we hoped somehow to find clues at least, if not actual directions, to where our loved ones might be held.

But where we found a lot more than we ever expected.

11

Julia went on being surprising when she ignored both the bus station and a taxi firm and found a place to hire a car. I'd never thought of that because, of course, I couldn't drive. Being stuck at fourteen, I guessed I'd never have that particular privilege.

Julia seemed to be a good driver, as she was good at lots of things that I'd never realized. It was a small car, not costing much to hire, but it felt like luxury, giving us priceless freedom and privacy that buses and taxis never could.

We trundled away, along a winding back road that kept our speed down. And so did the weather. A grey overcast sky had gathered early on, settling down towards the land. And since that region was totally flat farmland close to the sea, it produced its own greyness. Only thin and patchy, but still – mist.

After the Downward Path I never wanted to see a mist again. But it was hard to avoid in this soggy island, even in spring. So I gritted my teeth and kept my eyes on the road ahead, telling myself that it was just mist, not creepy at all.

Julia somehow guessed my feelings. 'At least there are no ghosts or demons in these mists.'

'We're heading for a Cartel house,' I said through my teeth. 'We don't *know* what might be skulking around.'

'But the mist will help us do our own skulking,' she said.

Then I was flung forward as Julia gasped and swerved the car to the edge of the road. A dirty green van with a dented door was booming past us on the narrow road, overtaking dangerously close to us.

Julia spat an unladylike word as the van roared on, disappearing around a misty curve. 'Crazy drivers might kill us before the Cartel has a chance,' she said.

'Worse than crazy,' I said unhappily. 'I got a quick look at the driver. The last time I saw him, you were tying him up and bandaging his arm.'

Neither of us had to spell it out. The two thugs had clearly got free and away from the guest house before the police or anything else could slow them down. And I had no doubt that they were on their way to the same place as us. To tell their Cartel 'master' all about us.

So, at last, the Cartel would know that we were alive. And, worse, they'd know roughly where to start looking for us.

Here we go again, I thought. There *will* be monsters in the mist before long.

Julia gave me an edgy look. 'We can't give up, Nick. We can't turn and run.'

I nodded. We could run, I thought, as someone once said, but we couldn't hide . . . 'We'll be in real danger now, wherever we go. And it shouldn't occur to them to start looking for us at Doul's house.'

That put us back into our usual silence. After a good while of quiet travelling, we got to the fringe of a pretty village where Headley Hall was to be found. It stood in plain sight on a small rise just beyond the village on the far side.

It was a tall, elegant building, all pale stone and dark wood, with beautifully kept grounds – and beyond them a lush meadow on one side and leafy woodland on the other. In sunlight it would look like something you'd see on a postcard. As it rose out of the thin drifts of mist, it looked like a trailer for a horror film.

I shook my head, trying to get a grip. 'We could probably get fairly close if we go through the woods.'

Julia nodded. 'And leave the car some place where we can get to it in a hurry.'

Since we didn't know what to expect, we had no real plan. It didn't seem a good idea to march up and knock on Doul's front door, so we aimed to sneak around and watch the place, learn what we could.

I wasn't sure what we'd do then. Maybe stop sneaking around and start trying to sneak *in*. And wouldn't that be fun, I thought, with who knows how many sorcerers and psychics Doul had with him in there.

And after that we'd face the problem of getting out . . .

Oh well, I thought. This trip had to end sometime.

Julia found a bumpy farm track leading up behind the woods, then turned through an open gate on to the edge of a field and tucked the car behind some bushes. Then we slipped into the misty dimness of the woods, where I led the way because sneaking around was one of my specialities. The dampness muffled any risk of swishing dry grass or crackling twigs and leaves underfoot, so we moved fairly noiselessly.

We found no fences or other barriers in the woods, and while there was some risk of magical protection I didn't think it was very great. Doul would have simpler ways of dealing with any local intruders.

So before long we were huddled behind a large bush, with a good view of one side of the house and a bit of the grounds at front and back.

Giving us a clear view of the green van with its dented door, standing on the smooth gravel driveway.

As I'd thought. The two minor-psychic thugs were reporting to Doul. I hoped they choked on whatever 'reward' he gave them.

Then I twitched at Julia's soft hiss. A number of oddly dressed people were coming into view from the back of the house.

At least they looked like people, but it was hard to be sure. They wore a sort of uniform – short loose tunics with hoods shadowing their faces, the cloth glinting as if it was metallic. They also all wore thick, coarse long-sleeved shirts underneath, and leggings of the same stuff, strangely extending over their hands and feet like gloves and socks.

I had no doubt that they were Doul's guards, since many carried light javelins and the rest had long, slim swords in their hands.

And they were searching.

I think we both stopped breathing as we watched them peer into every decorative shrub at the side of the house, behind every petal in the flower beds. Other guards like them could be seen at the back of the house, going through several outbuildings – sheds, barns, whatever – with the same care.

There weren't many of them – two squads of six guards each. Doul clearly didn't have a small army protecting his stately home. But that was the only good news, as Julia and I looked at each other, tense and puzzled.

We'd expected that what the two thugs had reported might start Doul looking for us. But he was doing just what I'd said he wouldn't do. *Starting* the search for us in his own backyard.

Poised to move away, we waited a moment – just long enough to see someone step out on to an ivy-covered balcony, through tall glass doors opening from a room on the second floor. The someone was very tall and narrow, with snowy white hair worn long, a trim white moustache, an elegant white suit and shoes. Even the skin of his long hands and face was bloodless white, giving an eerie ghostly effect.

And the person who followed the spooky man on to the balcony was even more scary. And more familiar. Black-haired, in a long black coat, with a fanged horned devil-face where lurid shades of blue and green rippled and shifted endlessly.

Kannis, the Cartel's leading sorcerer.

But then a third person came to join them, and I nearly cried out.

Small, slim, female, with long brown hair, wearing a plain white dress. April – following behind the two men. Not held or forced in any way that I could see, just walking quietly along like a docile, obedient child.

Or . . . like a slave.

12

I was vaguely aware of Julia, tense and trembling beside me, making a sound like a soft, high-pitched moan. But I didn't look at her. I was too busy with my own paralysing storm of shock and fright and bafflement, mixed with gladness at seeing that April was still alive.

But why was she there, like that? Keeping company with Kannis and the ghostly man who must be Doul? Looking so untroubled?

In fact we weren't close enough to see their faces clearly, nor to hear Kannis's words when he turned and spoke to her. And though every atom of me wanted to get closer – to rush wildly to her rescue – the small, hard survivor bit of me kept me still and silent, watching.

I told myself fiercely that they couldn't have *already* somehow corrupted April to make her their obedient slave. I had to believe that, or I'd have gone berserk. So it had to be that she was being *controlled,* magically.

Anyway, I planned to find out. Because now there

was even more reason to find a sneaky way into Doul's house.

But not right then. As we stood and stared, the group of hooded guards that had been looking under bushes turned towards the balcony, and one of them raised his hands and shrugged. I didn't need to hear his words to know he was reporting that nothing had been found.

And I didn't need to hear Doul's words when he pointed towards the woods where we were hiding, sweeping one long, dead-white hand to indicate the whole breadth of that small forest.

'He's told them to search the woods,' Julia whispered. She'd got her trembling under control, though she was still almost as pale as Doul.

'So we'll come back when they're finished,' I muttered.

We faded back into the woods, moving as swiftly as the need for silence allowed, and got back to the car that was as we'd left it, tucked behind the bushes just off the farm road.

When we got quietly into the front seat, we sat there for a moment, trying to gather ourselves, trying to come to terms with what we'd seen.

'They probably put some sort of command spell on her,' I said.

'Or it could be some kind of mind-clouding drug,'

Julia murmured. So she too was refusing to believe that April might have been wholly enslaved.

And then a voice spoke from the back seat.

'I fear,' it said, 'that her situation may be far worse than any of that.'

The shock made Julia cry out, made me jump and reach for the knife. But as we whirled we both realized that we knew that voice.

It was the mellow, stagy, caramel voice of the actor and mage we'd met on the Path, Bertrand Nowell.

He looked no different – still in his long-sleeved robe with the heavy hood, smiling a hopeful smile. But I knew that his face and hands, the only visible parts of him, were an illusion. Behind that, beneath the robe, he was a living skeleton – thanks to the evil of the Cartel.

'What are *you* doing here?' Julia demanded, looking furious.

'And what do you mean about April's "situation"?' I wanted to know.

'I'm looking for my body,' he said, answering Julia first. After turning him into a skeleton, and before sending him to the Path, the Cartel had kept his body for some reason. 'But why are you here, just the two of you?'

'Fray said that the Cartel captured you . . .' I said, ignoring his question.

'And that you betrayed us!' Julia snapped. 'Telling them we'd escaped the Path!'

I knew Bertrand was an actor and his face wasn't real, but his look of utter shock was fairly convincing. '*Betrayed?*' he repeated. 'Never! Do you really think I'd be stupid enough to make any *contact* with them? I'd have been back on the Path in an instant, or worse! Fray lied to you . . .'

That seemed plausible. After all, it wouldn't be the first time – the Cartel and truthfulness didn't exactly go hand in hand – but Julia still scowled.

'I wonder,' she said. 'It was very soon after you ran out on us that the Cartel knew we were back in this world.'

'Ah.' Bertrand looked suddenly uncomfortable. 'When I left you to look for my body, I began using a number of seeking spells and the like. And it's possible that one of those . . . *intrusions* . . . was spotted by the Cartel. When they discovered I'd left the Path, they no doubt suspected you had as well.'

'So it *is* your fault!' Julia raged. 'Everything that happened – Paddy and April and Sam being taken – is because of *you*!'

'Julia,' I said, as Bertrand looked shocked again, 'if it happened as he says, it was bad luck. And Sam did say it was only a matter of time before the Cartel found us. Bertrand is a pain and a prat, but he's not the enemy.'

'Oh, thank you very much, I'm sure,' Bertrand muttered.

Julia turned away. She'd always disliked and mistrusted Bertrand more than any of us did, I thought, and she didn't look like changing her mind.

'I *am* sorry,' Bertrand told me, 'if my searching brought harm to you. How were your friends "taken"? And how did you two get away?'

'Long story,' I said. 'Right now I want to know why you're here – and, most of all, what you meant about April.'

'Of course,' Bertrand said. 'But first we might find a safer place . . .'

So Julia, tight-lipped and silent, aimed the car back towards the village, while Bertrand talked.

'I actually managed to sneak into the house, just before dawn,' he said. 'Doul clearly doesn't think he needs a lot of security. My ESP made me aware of your April while I was inside, and I had a glimpse of her this morning, nothing more. I can't be certain, but it did seem that sadly she is no longer . . . herself. She seems like a robot or a zombie, and I doubt if it's a command spell or a drug. It's more as if the Cartel has altered her mind, stifling her will and her personality.'

That silenced Julia and me. We had no idea how that could be done or what could be done about it, if we ever had a chance to help her. And Bertrand hadn't seen enough of her to suggest anything.

So he tried to distract us from our gloomy silence by telling us about the earlier stages of his search – how his seeking spells had slowly narrowed things down until he was sure that his unoccupied body was being kept in Doul's manor house.

He had travelled slowly, using both magic and stealth to keep his weird, cloaked self unnoticed. And he'd lurked around Doul's house for several days, studying it. Then he did his magical burglary act and sneaked in.

But he was stopped when he ran into one of the strange guards prowling the dark corridors. Bertrand flattened him with some hasty magic and ran, but somehow an alarm was raised. He managed to get to the edge of the woods, and crept slowly away while the guards searched the house and the grounds – by which time we'd arrived.

'I got an ESP sense of you both, as I fled,' he said. 'Quite a surprise – but it was no time to start looking for you. And then I found this car, and sensed it was yours, so I waited.' He gave Julia a sharp look. 'If I'd actually "betrayed" you before, do you think I would have stayed around now to speak to you?'

'Yes,' Julia snapped. 'If you saw some advantage to yourself.'

'I don't understand all this hostility . . .' Bertrand began.

But I'd had a thought that was more important. 'You know,' I said, 'with your body here, Bertrand, and Kannis here, with *April* . . . Could it be that Doul's house is actually the Cartel headquarters?'

That got Julia interested. 'Did your ESP get any glimpse of Paddy and Sam as well?' she asked.

'Or of the Head of the Cartel?' I asked.

'I didn't sense your two friends,' Bertrand said, 'but they might just have been out of my reach. My ESP isn't strong . . . And I wouldn't know the Head of the Cartel if I saw him.'

'You wouldn't want to,' I muttered, and told him as quickly as I could about that terrifying scene when the Head had filled the sky with its monstrosity.

Bertrand was so horrified that the illusion of his face wavered, showing the empty-socketed skull beneath. 'A disembodied *Head*? Oh, gods . . .'

'What?' I asked.

'I've heard . . . things about the Cartel's master,' he muttered. 'That his immense power is possibly not human . . . And that despite his power he is not *whole*, in some frightful way, and takes brutal enjoyment in taking *wholeness* away from others . . . As he no doubt ordered Kannis to disembody me . . . And now – now I think I know what has made your April the way she is. They have removed her very *soul* from her body!'

13

I felt shocked, unable to speak, while Julia sat white-faced and blind with tears. Of all the vile, sadistic acts of Cartel magic that I'd run up against, that seemed the worst. To take anyone's soul seemed horrible enough. But *April's* . . .

'I'm very sorry,' Bertrand murmured, 'but I don't think I'm wrong. It's much like what was done to me, putting my spirit and inner self into this form. Except they have clearly kept her body active . . .'

And put her soul into some other form? I didn't want to think about that. 'So her body that we saw is sort of a zombie, like you said.'

'Not really,' Bertrand said. 'Those are reactivated corpses. The body you saw is alive, though it's a mostly empty vessel. It may have kept a few functions and abilities, but I can't guess which ones or how many . . . The thing is, it's as convenient a vessel as any and I expect once they've crushed her soul, they intend to reunite the physical with the mental or, shall we say, spiritual, so they can utilize her powers. I expect part of the reason for keeping them separate at the moment is for our benefit. They know you want the whole package—'

'And we'll get it,' Julia broke in suddenly. I saw that her tears had vanished, and her eyes had that steely glint again. 'And we'll find out if Paddy and Sam are in there too.'

Bertrand stared at her with disbelief. 'How? Do you think you can just stroll in?'

'You got in,' I pointed out. 'And you said Doul didn't have much security.'

'He may have tightened things up now, after my venture,' Bertrand said. 'And I got in using magic.'

'So use your magic to help us,' I said.

The illusion of his face wavered again as he drew back. 'I don't know about that . . .'

'Just get us in,' Julia said, the steeliness in her voice as well. 'Then use your magic again to locate April as well as your body. If you help us get to her, we'll help you find what you're looking for.'

He frowned, then nodded slowly. 'That might work. Just don't expect me to join you in some hopeless suicidal *battle*.'

Julia looked at me silently, and I shrugged and nodded. I wasn't sure how much help she'd really give Bertrand, but all that mattered to me was getting in and finding April. With Bertrand we had a chance.

Probably not much of a chance, I thought, but then Julia and I never had much of a chance from the moment we started out. We might get lucky in Doul's house, we might get killed. It didn't seem to matter.

April was in there, and we were going in to find her.

We got some food, and drove to a secluded spot outside the village to eat it, although, when it came to it, we weren't really hungry. And then we settled down in the car and tried to rest, though we weren't really tired either. But we felt we ought to be preparing ourselves for what we'd try to do when night finally came.

And seeing, every moment, the image of the obedient, submissive, soulless thing that April had been turned into.

Twilight seemed to take a long time to arrive, but it was getting usefully dark when we put the car back in its previous hiding place and set off through the trees. The knife, with its blade partly covered to reduce its silvery glow, gave enough light to get us through the forest's lightless depths. So we went quickly and quietly.

And no one was surprised that before long, as we got close to that Cartel house, the knife's glow turned golden.

At the edge of the woods we paused, and I sheathed the knife as we studied the big house. We saw lights in many windows, and I knew the big front door would be firmly locked. But I saw none of the strange hooded guards, and nothing else that looked like defences against intruders.

But then Bertrand reminded me that I wouldn't see any if they were magical.

'It seems that Doul is expecting me to try again,' he whispered, looking unhappy. 'He's put alarm spells on the doors and windows.'

'But no guards,' I muttered.

'They'll probably be on full alert inside,' he said.

'But how many are there?' Julia breathed. 'We just saw twelve, when they were searching. If there are more, Doul would surely have sent them out to search too.'

Twelve guards would be better than twenty, but still worrying enough. Though what Julia said seemed to brighten Bertrand.

'It's a very large place for not many guards,' he said, looking thoughtful. 'And I don't sense any other magics on the outside. Let's get closer, so I can see if I might get around one of the alarm spells or something.'

I hesitated, not liking the idea of crossing the open area of the grounds between the forest and the house. Even in that moonless darkness, someone might see our movement.

'Don't worry,' Bertrand said, seeing me draw back. He moved a hand quickly. 'There – I've put a little veiling spell on us in case anyone's looking out of a window. Come on.'

And with that we moved out of the forest and started towards the house.

14

We moved in a sort of crouching scuttle, vibrating with tension at being out in the open. But Bertrand's veiling magic must have worked, because nothing happened, no alarm was raised.

In seconds that seemed to take forever, we got into the shadows beside the house, by a side door that was probably for servants and tradesmen. And home invaders, I thought.

But then Bertrand stopped us. 'I don't like this,' he whispered. 'These spells are stronger than I expected, all of them. I won't find a way past them without setting off the alarms.'

I looked up, past the second-floor balcony where we'd seen April with the two sorcerers. There were several floors above that, plenty of windows, most of them in darkness. 'Are you sure that every window is covered by a spell?'

Bertrand shrugged. 'It's very likely. Though of

course I haven't looked at *every* window. There're dozens . . .'

'Then let's look,' Julia said firmly.

She gave Bertrand a little push, and he knew better than to argue. With a sigh, he set off – in a crab-like sideways shuffle, staying as close to the wall of the house as possible. Julia followed, and I shook my head and started after them, hoping there were no holes in the veiling spell.

In that way we crept around to the back of the house, pausing quite often while Bertrand used his magic to check on windows and another door.

But every time, he just shook his head and on we went.

Until we reached the other side of the house, the side furthest from the forest. When Bertrand stopped suddenly, craning his neck to stare upward.

'Wouldn't you know it,' he murmured sourly. 'Doul *has* left a few windows unguarded . . .' He pointed. 'See those small narrow ones, just under the eaves?'

We peered through the darkness, barely making out the small unlit rectangles.

'I suppose he knew it would be safe enough,' Bertrand said. 'My powers don't extend to flying, or even levitation. We can't get up there.'

I brushed my fingertips across the wall of the house. Climbing was one of my hard-won specialities. I'd climbed just about everything, from trees to drainpipes to old brick walls. And this house was made of stone that was *very* old, with lots of chips and crevices for fingertips and toes.

'I can,' I said.

Julia gave me a hopeful look, but Bertrand shook his head. 'It's a long way down if you fall.'

'Oh, right, I could be killed,' I muttered. 'I'd better stay here where we're all perfectly safe. Maybe we could ring the doorbell instead.'

'But I'm not sure I could keep you veiled, up there, and us as well,' Bertrand began.

I cut him off. 'Just veil yourselves. No one will see me.'

'Very well,' he sighed. 'If you do manage to get in, we'll go back to that door on the side facing the woods. If you can get to it, open it. The alarm spells won't be set off when it's opened from the inside.'

I nodded, and managed a twitch of my mouth that was as close as I could get to a reassuring smile. Then I reached up, found a fingerhold and started climbing.

Even in darkness it wasn't all that hard. That sort of climbing is all about keeping your concentration, one fingerhold and toehold at a time. Don't look down, don't look up, don't let yourself feel the strain and pain in hands and arms and backs of legs, don't think about how far you still have to go or how far you have to fall . . .

Definitely don't think about the risk of being discovered by a power-crazed sorcerer.

After a lifetime or two, I found to my surprise that there was a thin stone windowsill just above my right hand. A moment later I'd pulled myself higher, braced my elbows on the sill, and was warily studying the low, narrow window – and the blank darkness beyond it.

It was a casement window, opening on hinges like a small glass door. And it had better open, I thought. I really didn't feel up to climbing back down again.

Slowly, carefully, I reached down and drew the knife. Its golden glow shed a dim light on the small latch as I prised away at it.

It wasn't fastened. The window swung open smoothly, and as I sagged with relief I almost lost my grip on the sill.

Bertrand had said that Doul wasn't all that security-conscious. Like the rest of the Cartel, he obviously believed he was invincible. Still, if his overconfidence helped me, I wasn't going to complain.

With some struggling, I managed to heave myself up and over the sill. Rubbing my aching arms and legs, I stared around. The knife showed me a room that was small, low-ceilinged and oddly bare. Just four small, flat beds, child-size, a plain wooden table and two heavy wooden chests.

I couldn't imagine who would sleep in such a room. Did Doul keep children as slaves? I didn't know, didn't want to find out. All I wanted was to find a safe way down to that side door.

After listening hard at the closed door of the room, I opened it a bit at a time and peered out. A dark, deserted corridor stretched away past more closed doors, its walls as blank as those of the little room.

Gripping the knife so that only a sliver of light showed, I crept silently away along the corridor.

15

I'd sneaked around a lot of places where I shouldn't have been, in my years of living rough. But this was different – sneaking around a house that held two terrifying sorcerers, a number of armed guards and who knew what other dangers.

So though it was a warm night – even warmer on that less airy upper level of the house – I could feel droplets of cold sweat trailing down my spine.

But in fact I found that invading a sorcerer's home was made a bit easier in at least one way. It was a very old house, but Doul's magic kept every bit of it in near-perfect condition. Though that corridor was only bare floorboards, they were smooth and firm and polished, and not one of them squeaked under my feet.

And when I found a stairway – backstairs for servants, I thought, since it was as narrow and dark and blank as the corridor – its bare boards stayed just as silent. And so did I, as I drifted noiselessly downward.

But then I halted, suddenly seeing a problem. I

wasn't sure how high up I was. I'd looked up at the looming side of the house before I started climbing, but I wasn't sure how many levels there'd been up to the little windows under the eaves.

Was I five storeys up? Or six? Or more? I wasn't sure – and I got more confused as I tried to remember, tried to work it out.

I'd have to leave the stairway when I got lower, I thought. And find a window to look out of, to see what floor I was on. And find a way to the other side of the house. And not get caught . . .

Good-sized landings on the narrow stairway showed where each new level was as I crept down. After I'd got past four of them, I thought it was time to risk finding a window.

The door from the stairs was as free of creaks as the floor as I opened it a crack.

On the other side I saw a lushly carpeted corridor with a framed painting on the wall and a slim little table holding a decorative lamp that gave a soft pale light.

It was all totally silent. Let them all be soundly asleep, I thought. Let them all be totally certain that no one could possibly ever find a way into their amazingly well-guarded house.

Then I pushed the door wider, and slipped out on to the carpet. And everything stayed totally silent as I crept forward.

That floor of the house, and probably all the others, was something of a maze of interconnecting corridors with heavy panelled doors along every one. I had a very bad moment when one corridor led me to a wide, ornate, curving stairway, probably leading down to some kind of hall at the front door, from where I heard a faint clank of metal and low growling voices.

The speakers were too far away for me to make out words, but at least they didn't sound troubled in any way, and they weren't coming upstairs. Even so, I got away from the stairs as fast as I could. And the next connecting corridor looked likely to take me over to the side of the house where Julia and Bertrand were – I hoped – waiting.

Time to find a window, and work out how many more levels down I'd have to go. Holding my breath, keeping the knife ready, I clenched my teeth and opened one of the big polished doors.

I stepped through into silence with no threat or outcry from anywhere, closed the door behind me and started breathing again. I'd clearly found Doul's library, since there were high bookshelves on every wall, plenty of soft, comfortable chairs and sofas. There was a small light burning on a low side table, but no sign of anyone doing a bit of night-time reading.

And on the far wall I saw two tall glass doors, with heavy curtains pulled across them, which looked very much like the doors that led on to the second-floor balcony where we'd seen the two sorcerers and April.

I'd taken only one step in that direction when, behind me, the door from the corridor suddenly opened.

Whirling about, I saw a young man in shirtsleeves standing in the doorway, open-mouthed, goggling at me.

He was older than me, probably early twenties, but about the same height and quite skinny. He had mousy brown hair already getting sparse, a narrow face and watery eyes behind large glasses that perched on his long nose.

The eyes, fixed on the golden glow of the knife, filled with shock and fear. As his pinched mouth opened to cry out, his hands lifted as if to work some magic.

But panic turned his cry into a croak and made his hands tremble, messing up the spell. And as I bared my teeth and leaped at him, he squeaked and turned to run.

He wasn't fast enough. But even so, I didn't use the knife. It seemed too vicious to stab him in the back as he ran, and anyway I didn't want to leave a lot of tell-tale blood around the place. Instead, I clamped an arm around his throat and squeezed, to knock him out.

But he'd started twisting somehow, and the bones in his spindly frame must have been extra fragile. I heard a muffled *snap*, and he went limp in my grip, head lolling as it does when the neck is broken.

I quickly dragged his body all the way into the library and closed the door. He was thin enough to be stuffed under a sofa that stood against the wall so that he was fully hidden.

'Damn!' I muttered, scowling at the place where he lay. 'Should have made him take me to April.'

Then I jerked wildly, almost yelling with shock as another voice broke the room's silence. A soft voice that I knew, yet sounding weirdly flat and lifeless.

'April is not here,' the voice said.

But she was.

16

I whirled round, and froze. She was sitting quietly in the depths of a big chair, where she must have been all along. She wore the same dress that I'd seen before, her long hair was glossy and bright as ever, her large hazel eyes were still luminous . . .

But different. The eyes that I was staring at were blank and empty, as lifeless as her voice had been.

As *soulless.*

'I am not April,' she said. 'This is April's body and some parts of her mind. The real April is . . . elsewhere.'

'Where?' I croaked.

'Another big house,' she said. 'I do not know where it is.'

I went on staring. 'Will you . . . Are you going to raise the alarm?'

'Only if you wish it,' she said. 'I can do only what I am told to do.'

That *really* wasn't like April, I thought. But it unclenched my stomach to know that this blank, docile

April wouldn't betray me – and would answer questions.

'Who and what was that?' I asked, nodding towards the corpse under the sofa.

'His name is Jenz,' she said. 'He is one of Mr Doul's young persons that he calls his juniors.'

My heart sank. 'One of'? Was the whole place crawling with young sorcerers who might not all be as feeble as Jenz?

'How many are there?' I asked.

'One other,' she said. 'Younger than Jenz. I think her name is Stoll.'

My heart lifted a little. Just one, and young. I hoped she was having a good sleep.

'How did you get here?' I asked. 'And *why* are you here?'

'Mr Kannis brought me, by magic,' she said. 'I do not know why.'

I had so many questions I could barely think straight, especially when I knew it wasn't the best time to ask them. But some had to be asked.

'In that other big house,' I said quickly, 'are Paddy and Sam there too? And is the *Head* there?'

She didn't move or blink or show the slightest trace of a feeling. 'Paddy and Sam are there,' she said. 'Their souls, their real selves, have also been removed and put into other bodies. And the great Head is there. Though sometimes the one that lives within it is not there.'

Paddy and Sam in different bodies? Some mysterious 'one' living inside the Head? The new shocks nearly knocked me off my feet. They also raised about a thousand more questions. But they'd have to wait.

'Can you take me down to the side door facing the woods, and open it?' I asked. 'Without letting anyone see or hear us.'

'If you wish it,' she said. And she quietly got up and led the way.

That took us back into the house's maze of shadowy corridors and silent closed doors. But April seemed to know the way, and obediently stayed alert in case anyone came along. So we only had two scary moments along the way.

The first was when we hid in a darkened alcove while two strange figures went past. One was a pudgy girl in her late teens with straggly blonde hair and a round spotty face, wearing a baggy purple robe. The other was child-size and not all human, wearing only a short skirt or kilt. Its face was pointed with large eyes and ears and a tiny mouth, and all of its visible skin was covered in short grey fur.

When they'd gone past, I risked a whispered question.

'The human is the other junior, Stoll,' April told me.

'The other one is one of the servitors. They do not speak. Mr Doul likes his house to be quiet.'

I was all too ready to fit in with that house rule. And just as well, when the second scary moment sent us dodging back around a corner while one of the hooded guards came down some stairs. But even as we hid, I had a glimpse of the guard. He too was only partly human, with the head and face of a large cat, like a panther, with slanted yellow eyes and dangerous fangs. All his visible skin, too, was covered in dark fur, which I'd mistaken for cloth when I'd seen the guards earlier.

'One of the watchmen,' April whispered.

Servants like mice, guards like cats . . . It might have been Doul's idea of a joke. But cats have excellent hearing, can see in the dark and are lethal hunters.

After that we walked even more carefully. But when we stopped a third time we might have started tap-dancing and still not been heard.

Through an open door I heard the voices of two men who didn't seem to be having a friendly chat. One voice I knew – the ugly rasping tones of the devil-faced sorcerer, Kannis. The other voice was clipped, slightly high-pitched and almost comically plummy. It wasn't hard to work out that it belonged to the white-on-white owner of the house, Doul.

As I lurked in the dark corridor with April, listening, I would have been wide open to discovery by any passing cat-watchman. Luckily no one came along. And the risk was worth it, because the row the two mages were having was very revealing.

And terrifying.

17

'I have no choice!' Kannis was snarling as I began to listen. 'It was a direct *order* from the Head!'

'Surely you can explain to him,' Doul said, 'how circumstances have changed here, requiring your presence.'

Kannis snorted. 'I'm not *required*. You don't need my help against a single mage who is certainly not on your level of power.'

'Rather more than that, I think,' Doul said sharply, 'with the Changeless Boy being seen in the area. No doubt with magical allies.'

'It's far more likely,' Kannis sneered, 'that those two louts made up a story to win your favour.'

Doul's voice was icy. 'The "louts" described him clearly – and in any case they would not dare lie to me.'

'They described a youth with a big shiny knife,' Kannis sniffed. 'Doul, I *saw* the boy dying in Fray's absurd desert.'

'But you didn't see him *dead*,' Doul pointed out.

'And you know his powers of recovery. He has always been exceedingly hard to kill. And he has managed to do a great deal of damage to the Cartel, including the loss of Fray and Redman. Indeed, I think of him as rather like a chemical catalyst, whose presence causes turmoil—'

'Forget chemistry!' Kannis barked. 'Even if he still lives, you should remember that he is mostly Powerless. And you have no reason to assume he has *allies*.'

'The very fact that he has found his way *here*,' Doul rasped, 'indicates that he has been helped!'

Silence fell for a moment, and I had the happy thought that the two might be quietly strangling each other. But then Kannis spoke again.

'Perhaps that is so,' he growled. 'But he and his allies haven't moved against you. And if they do, you can always contact the island for help. You might also do something about your foolishly weak defences.'

'They are strong enough,' Doul said, suddenly sounding weary. 'And you're well aware that I prefer a quiet life, as a thinker and a scholar rather than a man of *action*. I don't want a host of other mages, an army of watchmen . . . I hate all that sort of *fuss*. Indeed, I wish you'd never brought the girl's body here in the first place. Or that other body.'

'Nowell's body can stay,' Kannis snarled. 'I still hope to corrupt and recruit him, after he has been tormented a while longer – and we both know that the Head might kill the body on a whim. And I still believe that I was right to bring the girl's body away from the island, to avert disaster.'

'But surely now that you've been ordered to return it,' Doul said, 'you're risking that disaster again!'

'That's as may be,' Kannis muttered. 'But now that the Head is back again, it's not my decision – or yours. He wants the girl's body *there* – perhaps to use as some kind of threat. Or, for all I know, simply for the pleasure of *destroying* it, to avoid complications.'

Doul sighed. 'When will you leave?'

'At once,' Kannis said. 'After I have gathered my things – and collected the girl's body from wherever it is.'

That seemed to mean that the talking was over, and I beckoned to April and got us away from there before Kannis came out of the room. As we crept away, my mind felt as if it was bulging with new mysteries and questions.

I'd grimly enjoyed listening to Doul's testimonial to me, though I wasn't sure what a 'catalyst' was. And it was good to know that Doul wasn't going to strengthen his security. But their talk of 'disaster', at wherever Kannis was taking April, filled me with anxiety.

And the idea that the Head might idly destroy April's body scared me rigid.

It didn't seem to bother her though. As we crept quickly away, her calm, blank face showed no sign of distress or any other feeling at what she'd heard.

Just as it showed no sign of joy when we finally got to the side door and let Julia and Bertrand inside.

I could see that Julia wanted to hug April. But, like me, she held back. The being who stood gazing emptily at us, waiting for instructions, wasn't April. It would have been like hugging a shop-window mannequin.

As urgently as I could, I related some of what I'd heard in the row between the two sorcerers. 'We have to get away, *fast*!' I whispered. 'Before Kannis takes her back to wherever they came from . . .'

Bertrand's face twisted, the skull showing. 'But I have to find my *body*!' he said desperately.

'Do what you like,' Julia snapped. 'We're taking April out of here.'

'You said you'd *help* me!' Bertrand pleaded.

That made me hesitate. I knew what Julia meant, but I also knew that her hostility to Bertrand was a bit over the top. He hadn't betrayed us, we wouldn't have got to April without him and we did say we'd help.

'Julia, you take April to the car,' I said. 'I'll help Bertrand find his body. I think we owe him . . .' An obvious thought suddenly hit me. 'April, do you know where in the house his body might be?'

Her voice was as toneless as ever. 'After Bertrand tried to get in last night, Mr Doul went down to the cellars. He said it was to check on the body.'

When I asked, she pointed to a dim, narrow side passage that led to the stairs down to the cellars.

As simple as that.

Julia still looked angry, ready to argue with me, but there wasn't time.

'You have to take April.' I told her. 'It shouldn't take us long to search the cellars. We'll be right behind you.'

And Bertrand and I hurried away along the shadowed passage.

18

The stairs leading down were also narrow and plain and dark, but as usual the knife provided enough light. From the foot of the stairs another low passage led into more darkness. And as we edged along it, we came to a junction with passages leading away on either side.

April had spoken of 'cellars' – more than one: maybe a lot more, I thought. Maybe we wouldn't be as close behind Julia as I'd hoped.

But I'd forgotten about Bertrand's powers. He wasn't going to use a spell there, in the enemy's house, but he still had his short-range ESP. When he raised a shaking hand to point to the left-hand passage, his excitement made the illusion vanish so that the hand was white bone.

'*There*,' he whispered. 'Some place along there . . . My body . . . So near . . .'

The knife's glow showed several heavy doors on either side of the passage ahead. But as we moved forward Bertrand flinched, glancing back. 'Someone's coming,' he hissed. 'On the stairs.'

Grateful for that ESP warning, more grateful that the nearest door wasn't locked, I pushed it open and pulled Bertrand inside, into a small windowless room. His body wasn't there, nor was much else except heaps of decorating stuff – tins of paint, buckets, ladders and so on.

And in his fright Bertrand managed to stumble over one of the tins.

The clank of a bony foot against the metal was just loud enough to be heard by whoever was coming our way. I saw the door starting to open, and we both dodged down behind a stack of paint tins. Carefully, because they'd been stacked carelessly and the lids were loose on many of them.

I sheathed the knife so the room would be lightless. But a dim glow came in as the door opened, as if a light had been turned on in the passage. It was enough to show two of Doul's cat-like watchmen prowling in, staring around, eyes gleaming . . .

Then their gaze locked on to the tins where we were crouching. They smiled, showing their fangs – and long, cruel, needle-sharp cat claws suddenly sprang out from the tips of their furry fingers.

'Run!' I yelled at Bertrand, and leaped up from

behind the tins. As I leaped I scooped up one of the tins and hurled it.

The two watchmen were also in mid-leap towards me when the loose lid came off the tin and about two litres of yellow paint hit them square in their grinning faces.

As they squalled, pawing at their paint-blinded eyes, Bertrand dashed wildly past them towards the door. I snatched up another tin – heavy, with a tight lid – and swung it twice at the watchmen's heads. And I was through the door before their unconscious bodies hit the floor.

In the passage I saw Bertrand's cloak disappearing through another doorway further along, and raced to join him. After all the cat-yowling of the two watchmen, I was desperately hoping that the cellars of Doul's house – which, I recalled, he liked to be kept 'quiet' – were fairly soundproof.

The room that Bertrand had entered looked like a general junk room – cluttered heaps of boxes, chests, old bits of furniture. But I barely glanced at it all.

Bertrand was standing in the middle of the room, quivering, making a small, high keening sound. Looking down at himself.

It looked like a corpse, half-covered by a sheet, sprawled on an old, thin mattress in a corner. But it had

Bertrand's face, and as I peered at it I could see that it was slowly breathing.

'Look!' Bertrand said, his shaky voice full of outrage. 'They've just *flung* me here, carelessly, like a piece of trash . . .'

'All right,' I said sharply. 'They're cruel and evil, we know that. Now do what you have to so we can get *out* of here.'

He twitched, blinked, then raised his hands and began muttering some magic spell.

I drifted back towards the door, nervously listening – and spotted a peculiar object in the corner. Not a box or a chest, but a tallish wooden cylinder like an old-fashioned umbrella holder.

But instead of umbrellas it held a cluster of old-style weapons, standing on end like weird flowers in a big vase. Swords of different sizes, a few short spears, all a bit old and rusty but serviceable.

I went to have a closer look, thinking a sword might come in handy if we met any more watchmen with claws . . .

And the door crashed open.

I was in the corner behind it, so I had time to duck down behind the container of weapons. I heard Bertrand gasp and saw him collapse to the floor, still conscious but lying stiffly as if held down by something unseen.

And then I saw Doul stalk in, with two more watchmen, their claws unsheathed.

The sorcerer was all white, as usual, and I was close enough to see that his eyes were also a blank and deathly white, though he wasn't blind. In that moment he seemed every bit as terrifying as Kannis ever had.

'I must say, you've done very well, getting into my house again,' he said, smiling down at Bertrand. 'But sadly for you, old chap, all that effort has been entirely in vain. I'm afraid that you won't be reclaiming that body. Not now – in fact, not ever.'

19

His plummy voice was smooth and nasty, like his smile. As he watched Bertrand writhing on the floor, both voice and smile held all the smug certainty of a top-level Cartel sorcerer who believes that he is totally in control and invincible.

But that arrogance and self-confidence often led the Cartel to make mistakes. Fray and Redman had done just that, and now so had Doul.

His poor security was one serious mistake. But also – because Bertrand had been alone the first time he'd tried to get into that dangerous place – Doul clearly never thought that anyone would be *with* Bertrand this time.

So, enjoying his capture, Doul wasn't checking for others.

He didn't know I was there.

And as that thought made me start bracing myself for a sudden move, I saw that Doul had made a third mistake.

He'd underestimated Bertrand.

Despite the spell that Doul had hit him with, Bertrand managed to find enough power of his own to break partly free from Doul's magic. Still on the floor, he gasped an angry word.

A burst of magical force appeared in mid-air, in the shape of a giant, pale blue blade, which slashed at Doul. The sorcerer leaped back with a shocked cry, his power blocking the blue blade just in time, which then vanished.

In that explosive moment, as the watchmen crouched and snarled, and both mages set themselves to strike again, I surged to my feet, grabbed a javelin from the container in front of me and threw it.

I'm no expert spear-thrower, but Doul was only a few paces away, hard to miss. And I wasn't bothered this time about attacking from behind.

The javelin drove into the middle of Doul's back. He staggered, shrieking with the sudden unexpected pain – and disappeared.

The two watchmen stood frozen with shock for an instant, as I snatched a handy sword and leaped at them. I swung the sword at the neck of the first one, and when he tried to dodge it, the blade bit deep into his skull.

As he fell, it got stuck. And before I could wrench it

free, the second watchman lunged, his claws going for my throat.

I twisted away, but the claws bit into my left shoulder. My left hand went numb. I lost my grip on the sword and couldn't reach for the knife. And the cat-monster's fangs and claws glittered as he leaped.

Until the centre of his torso silently exploded in a cloud of blood and torn flesh, and what was left of him collapsed on the floor.

Bertrand was on his feet, rejoining the fight just in time.

'Thanks,' I gasped.

'Same to you,' he said, with a skull-grin.

Then he turned back to his sprawled body on the mattress and went on with his spell as if he had all the time in the world.

'Bertrand . . .' I began, feeling some urgency as I imagined Doul on his way back with who knew what reinforcements.

But he didn't seem to be listening – and in fact I couldn't hear any sounds in the passage outside or anywhere else. Anyway, he needed no more than a minute or two to complete the magic.

I had no idea what to expect, so I jumped when his cloak suddenly vanished, leaving his skeleton shape fully in view.

Then the bones of the skeleton began to glow, as if

their solidity was turning into radiant light. With the last word of the spell, what had been the skeleton became glowing dust, which drifted to the floor and disappeared.

And the body on the mattress sat slowly up, blinking, gasping, peering down at itself.

I jumped again when the sheet that covered it suddenly turned into clothing – shirt, trousers, shoes, a slightly flash suede jacket.

'Now that is *worlds* better,' Bertrand said, getting to his feet. 'Body and spirit together, back as I should be . . .'

'But we shouldn't be *here*,' I said. 'Come on!'

My shoulder wound was mostly recovered, so I drew the knife as we rushed for the door and raced away. Bertrand the skeleton had only ever managed a slow lope, but Bertrand in his own body had a good turn of speed. We fled along the passage and up the stairs, and every step of the way I expected to meet a storming deadly attack by sorcery and watchmen.

But though I thought I heard distant cries in the house somewhere above us, no one got in our way. Maybe, I thought hopefully, Doul is dead or too badly injured to call for help – and he probably only had two watchmen left . . .

We saw nothing but darkness until we burst out of the side door and sprinted for the woods.

The knife's light let us keep up the pace and avoid running into trees as we ran on.

Bertrand was puffing and gasping a bit by then, and a moment later came to a sudden stop, doubled over.

'Stitch,' he panted. 'Wait . . .'

He turned towards the darkness behind us and moved his hands in a magic gesture, murmuring a few words.

'That'll veil our tracks and send pursuers the wrong way,' he said. 'Doul would be able to break through it, but I doubt if he'll come chasing through the forest after us. I think your spear hurt him badly, Nick. Maybe even killed him.'

'We can only hope,' I muttered. And we started off again.

A moment later the knife's glow showed that we'd entered a small open clearing among the trees. And there we came to a sudden stop.

On the far side of the clearing, mostly in shadow, we saw someone standing very stiff and still. Not a looming cat-warrior or white-clad sorcerer. Someone not very tall, someone who I realized was female – someone I knew . . .

'Julia!' I said, feeling icy anxiety clutch my stomach. She was alone. No slim long-haired girl beside her. '*Where's April?*'

'Gone,' Julia said, moving forward into the light,

looking more desolate than I'd ever seen her. 'She just . . . vanished, a short while after you left.'

The iciness inside me became a glacier. I heard Kannis's words again, telling Doul that he would 'collect' April – by magic, of course – and take her back.

Back to whatever unknown place of horror they were in before.

20

We reached the car safely, found it in one piece and undiscovered, then just sat in it for a few silent minutes. Julia was quivering with grief and rage over the loss of April, as if it was one loss too many. And I felt much the same. I kept reminding myself that it had just been April's empty, helpless body – but it might have led us to the real April.

At the same time I was trying to think about where Kannis could have taken that body. And as those positive thoughts started lifting me out of useless anger and despondency, I guessed they might do the same for Julia.

'We might find her again,' I said. 'I heard Doul and Kannis talking. Kannis said that he'd taken her away from *the island* – and that Doul could contact the island . . . Remember what Alderon told us . . .'

'You spoke with *Alderon*?' Bertrand, in the front seat beside Julia, turned to stare at me, looking impressed.

'He's Paddy's uncle,' I told him. 'And he said he'd

heard lots of mentions – when he was spying on the Cartel – of a special secret island, off the east coast.'

'But that's impossible,' Bertrand said. 'If it's off-shore, they'd have to cross salt water.'

'Maybe they've found a way to do it,' I said. 'Maybe the Head did some super-magic. Maybe they built a bridge—'

'That wouldn't work,' Bertrand said. 'You'd still be going over the water . . .'

I frowned. 'What if there's a sort of strip of land reaching out? A *land* bridge? What if they used magic to put a strip of land there?'

'Then it wouldn't be an island,' Bertrand said. 'It'd be a peninsula.' His mouth twisted in a half-smile. 'Actually, that might be suitable. Another word for a point of land jutting into the sea is . . . a Head-land.'

'Oh funny,' I snarled. 'The point is, from what I heard, Kannis and April and the Head had all been at that place, whatever it is. And that must be where April is now. Her body, anyway.'

Julia had stayed silent, and I'd thought she wasn't listening. But Bertrand's feeble joke had made her whip around to glare at him. Then she turned her glare on me.

'What does it matter if it's an island or not?' she cried. 'We don't have any idea where it *is*! And there are hundreds of miles of coastline!'

Bertrand nodded, looking apologetic. 'And they would have every kind of powerful veiling spell and the like, to keep it secret.'

'But we have to look for it,' I insisted. 'From everything else Kannis said, with the Head being there and everything, that place – whatever it is – has to be the Cartel's main base! Alderon told us that Kannis probably lived at the base, not in a house of his own like Redman and Doul . . .'

And the sudden, clear flash of an idea made me jump, so that they both turned and stared.

'If what I did just left Doul injured,' I said, 'he might need help. If he's badly hurt, or dead, someone *else* in that house might need help.' Quickly I told them about Doul's two juniors – the one I'd killed, and the pudgy girl named Stoll. 'If she needed help, she might well call to Kannis! She could be in magical contact with the Cartel base!' I grabbed Bertrand's no-longer-bony arm. 'Is there some magic that could *tap into* a call like that?'

He looked startled, then thoughtful. 'I don't have enough ESP to do that,' he said. 'But there's a form of magical *seeing*, called scrying . . . Using things like crystal balls and mirrors . . .'

He twisted the car's rear-view mirror towards himself and stared into it, muttering quick, lilting words. When I craned my neck to look, the mirror showed me only my own tense face.

But it showed Bertrand a lot more.

'I'm seeing a tubby blonde girl,' he breathed. 'I think the spell is showing me something that happened some minutes ago. The girl speaking to Kannis, asking for help, just as you thought. Ah, there – Doul is still alive, but barely. Your spear hit his spine, Nick, damaging his spinal cord . . .'

He jerked, then scowled. 'Kannis must have done some magic. Doul and the girl suddenly vanished.'

'Can you tell where they went?' Julia asked urgently.

Bertrand went on peering at the mirror. 'Kannis did a very powerful magic that made them move *instantly* to wherever it was. So it left no trail.'

For no reason, I thought of Sam Foss, talking once about 'backtracking' magic.

'But when the aide did her little magic, before, to *contact* Kannis,' Bertrand went on, starting to smile, 'my scrying spell is showing *where* she reached out to! Do you have a map?'

Julia pulled a road map out of a pocket in the car door. I drew the knife to give a light, and Bertrand peered at the map, still looking delighted.

'The scrying didn't pinpoint it exactly,' he muttered. 'Probably the Cartel's veils and protections got in the way. But it showed a general location – *there*.'

He pointed to the part of the map showing the

eastern coast. Then he ran his finger along a stretch of open shoreline between two good-sized villages.

As I leaned closer I could make out a tiny shape near his finger. An uneven shape that looked, on the map, not much bigger than a full stop.

Something just offshore, in the blue area of the map that indicated the sea.

Something like an island.

21

Without a word Julia started the car and drove away, her face and body taut with grim determination. And at the speed she was reaching on those dark back roads, I was glad I was in the back seat.

'Let's not get killed in a crash,' I said through my teeth, 'before the Cartel has a go at us.'

That slowed her down a little, though her expression and her silence didn't change. Not until Bertrand got a glimpse of an old signpost and looked puzzled.

'Do you know you're heading west?' he asked Julia. 'The sea coast is the other direction—'

'I know where I'm going,' Julia snapped.

That silenced us both. Clearly she didn't think it would be a good idea to charge wildly off, right then, to that bit of coastline where the island was. Probably she wanted to pause, and think, and plan a little.

Though I wasn't sure it would help. I wasn't sure how to *plan* for trying to sneak into the secret, hidden, protected Cartel headquarters without being noticed by the Head and Kannis and who knew what other enemies.

At the same time, I thought, it might help to know exactly who would be doing that sneaking.

'Bertrand,' I said carefully, 'are you staying with us? We could do with your magic when we get . . . where we're going.'

He frowned uneasily, silent for a moment, and Julia turned briefly to look at him. Her gaze still seemed a bit hostile, as it had all along – but there was something else in her eyes. Like hope, and desperation.

And Bertrand saw it too, and sighed. 'Good sense would tell me to go a long way away and try to hide – especially now that I've just got myself and my body together again. But I suppose there are no real hiding places if the Cartel wants to find me. And I feel strangely unwilling to turn away, to let you go on by yourselves.'

'So you'll come with us, and help us?' I said.

He sighed again. 'I'll come to the coast with you and help you look, and try to keep you out of sight. But I'm no warrior hero, Nick. I won't be marching along to die at your side when you launch some suicidal assault on the Cartel.'

'I'm not planning one,' I said. 'Anyway, you did the warrior thing pretty well in Doul's cellar.'

'That was mindless reflex,' he said, 'born of utter panic.'

As Julia sniffed, I went on before she could say something cutting. 'If you say so,' I told Bertrand. 'We'll be glad of whatever help you can give.' I offered a wry smile. 'And feel free to do a few more mindless reflexes, if we need them.'

Julia managed to keep our speed down as we rolled through the pretty village – all silent, dark, asleep, as unaware as ever of the truth about the big house that loomed over it. As we drove on, the sky behind us gathered a tinge of greyish-pink light as the night gave way to dawn. And I was glad to see the rising sun by the time we reached the small city where Julia and I had stayed.

With everything that had happened, it felt like an age since we'd first arrived there. I thought briefly about the two thugs who had attacked us, but it didn't seem likely that we'd run into them again in the very early morning. And if somehow we did, I thought, even they wouldn't be stupid enough to try anything on the street in broad daylight.

But they were.

Julia had taken us back to the city mainly to re-hire the car for a longer time, since she'd first taken it only for a day. And she dropped Bertrand and me off, with a good handful of cash, to pick up some food and water, to keep us going while we crept around the coast looking for the island.

When we were finished with that chore, Bertrand spotted an empty bench in a little park and decided he needed a rest. He was feeling sleepy in his reclaimed body, and enjoying the new summer sunshine. A lot better, as he said, than being a hooded skeleton in a clammy mist.

But I was too wound up for sitting and dozing in the sun. So I left him on the bench, with the bag of food, and went for a wander.

As I walked along in the sunshine I struggled to keep my head free of dark thoughts about what might happen to us when we reached the coast. I tried not to think that we'd be at a place where the Head wouldn't be far away; and Kannis; and April's soulless body . . .

And since I didn't seem to have anything else to think about, I tried hard to make myself stop thinking altogether, and just drift along in the moment.

And then the moment turned nasty.

I smelt them first – a wave of stale booze and smoke odours. Then I heard the growling voices, full of surprise and ugly laughter.

I turned, heart sinking, to see the two hulking minor-psychic thugs grinning at me.

They looked the worse for wear, beer-stained and swaying as if they'd been at the drink all night. But their mean little eyes looked alert enough – and their hands were steady as they produced their weapons, the combat knife and the short heavy club.

'Would y' believe it,' the club-wielder said. 'Here he is again.'

They moved apart and started towards me. I backed away, with nowhere to go but a dank little alleyway that smelt almost as bad as they did. Around me the early-morning streets were empty, and Bertrand was well out of sight.

'He won't get lucky this time,' the other one growled. 'We'll take him to the master in *pieces* if we have to.'

22

'You won't,' I said through my teeth. 'Doul is dead. And I killed him.'

I knew that might not be entirely true, since Bertrand's magic had discovered that Doul hadn't quite managed to die. And the thugs clearly didn't believe me.

'You?' sneered the one with the knife. 'You never got near him, or you wouldn't be standin' here.'

'Tear you apart in a second he would,' said the other.

'No,' I said. 'Not him, and *definitely* not you.'

That brought them lurching forward, growling, weapons raised.

There's nothing quite like the combination of fear and fury, the best performance-enhancing drug ever known. I drew the knife so fast it seemed to leap into my hand, and both of them hesitated for a moment at the sight of its golden glow in the alley's dimness.

It had been silvery when they saw it before. Because it was golden now, I knew that the two of them had been rewarded with some low-level positions in the Cartel. And the colour-change seemed to puzzle them a little.

So I swung the knife high, above my head. And when both their gazes dumbly followed its brightness, I took a fast step forward and kicked the club-wielder, hard, right between the legs.

He shrieked, doubled up and collapsed. In the same instant I swung the knife down again and slashed at the other one's jutting beer belly.

The slash was carefully gauged, since I wasn't planning to leave any bodies behind for the police or anyone to find. The golden blade cut through the thug's T-shirt as if it was tissue paper, but barely grazed the skin of his belly, leaving a line of blood like a thin red thread.

The thug stared down at himself, turned grey-white and fell over in a total faint.

And I took another step and kicked the first one in the head. My trainer didn't do him any serious damage – just stunned him, to silence his wheezing groans.

That was when Bertrand arrived, at a gallop, shopping bags in his hands.

'Nick!' he panted. 'I got an ESP sense you were in trouble . . .'

'No trouble,' I said.

He looked down at the two unconscious louts and smiled. 'Very restrained of you to leave them alive.'

'Wasn't it?' I agreed. 'Especially when they've been taken into the Cartel.'

His smile faded. 'Then let's not leave them at large.'

He set the bags down and moved a hand. The two thugs stirred, opened their eyes and struggled to their feet. I braced myself – but Bertrand spoke two strange, quiet words and both of them went still, standing slumped, gazing blankly straight ahead.

'Now,' Bertrand told them, 'you will leave here and have quite a lot more to drink. When you are staggering drunk, you will go to the main police station and throw large stones through its windows. Go.'

Obediently the two thugs marched away, out of the alley.

'Good one,' I said, grinning.

'It'll keep them out of mischief for some while, I imagine,' Bertrand said. 'Now let's find Julia before she decides to go and fight the Cartel on her own.'

In fact she was looking quite impatient when we got to the car-hire place, where she was sitting in the car, tapping her fingers on the steering wheel. But she calmed down when I explained about the two thugs, and she seemed to approve of our low-key way of handling them. She also more or less approved the food and things that we'd bought. She even managed a small smile.

And so, despite everything, all three of us were smiling as she started the car and set off for the seaside.

Julia drove more sedately this time, so it took a while to reach one of the coastal villages by the open stretch of shoreline that we'd seen on the map. There we found a parking lot with a sea view, where we brought out our store of food and had a tense and not very cheerful picnic, huddled in the car.

We realized that we hadn't really worked out what we'd do when we arrived at our destination. And we all felt the same weight of dread, from the awareness that the centre of the Cartel's evil power probably lay no more than a mile or two from where we were sitting.

'What troubles me,' Bertrand murmured, 'is the strong possibility that they'll be *expecting* us.'

'Will they though?' Julia asked. 'Those two louts may have told Doul about Nick and me being in the city back there, but the Cartel might just as easily think that was coincidence.'

'After our skirmish in Doul's house?' Bertrand asked.

Julia shook her head. 'You said that Nick threw the spear from *behind* Doul, who vanished. Even if he's still alive and able to speak, to tell them what happened, he only saw *you*, Bertrand.'

'Doesn't matter,' I muttered. 'April saw us all.' Julia turned with a startled frown and I went on. 'April's *body*, I mean. And she has to do as she's told. If they think to ask her, she'll tell them all about us.'

That stopped Julia, but only for a moment. 'But she doesn't know that we planned to come here. No one does. The Cartel won't imagine that we know anything about an *island*. And I really do think they'd never *imagine* that we'd ever come anywhere near their headquarters.'

Bertrand shook his head. 'There's a famous book – I forget who wrote it – on the art of war. Somewhere it says that a good general never plans for what he thinks the enemy *might* do. He plans for what he knows the enemy *can* do.' He sighed. 'The Cartel knows us – Nick and me anyway – knows how tenacious we've been in the past. They might think it's highly unlikely that we'd even find this place, let alone be foolish enough to come here. But they might also be planning an unpleasant welcome, just in case we do.'

23

It was a chilling thought, but since I'd had thoughts of my own along those lines, I didn't do much shivering. And though I knew nothing about books on the art of war, I saw that it made sense to plan for the unexpected.

Not that I had any idea how to make plans for facing the Cartel, since I couldn't even guess at the capability of the monstrous Head's power. But I knew something else that the Cartel was capable of.

Mistakes. Growing out of arrogance.

'Never mind generals,' I said to Bertrand. 'Whatever it feels like to us, the Cartel doesn't see this as a *war*. So they wouldn't be setting up any big defences or clever strategies. To them, dealing with us would just be pest control.'

Bertrand raised an eyebrow. 'Is that supposed to be reassuring, Nick?'

'It should be,' I said. 'All of them – their hunters and soldiers, the sorcerers on every level all the way up to

Kannis – have the same problem. And I'd bet anything the Head has it too. They think they're all-powerful, unbeatable. They think we're nobodies, not possibly a serious threat.'

'Perhaps they're not wrong,' Bertrand murmured.

'Doesn't matter,' I said. 'That book on war should've said something about overconfidence. It breeds mistakes, leaves openings.'

I took a deep breath. They were looking at me as if I was a commander giving instructions. All right, I thought – maybe I am.

'What we have to do now,' I went on, 'is look around as much as we can, watch and listen for any hints or clues about this island, *learn* whatever we can about it. At the same time we stay totally alert, all the time, day and night. We suspect everyone and everything until we've checked them out. We watch each other's backs, we take turns staying awake at night. In their arrogance they can lose concentration now and then, let their attention wander. We can't. Not for a second, not ever. And that way we might not only stay alive – we might find a weakness, an opening.'

Bertrand was looking a bit uneasy, as well as startled, but Julia was nodding.

'We should remember,' she told him, 'that this is the boy who has survived years of fighting demon stalkers, who has attacked its two most powerful sorcerers and lived to tell the tale.'

'I know,' Bertrand muttered. 'I've seen the young warrior in action. But I'm far from sure that he can so easily make warriors of *us*.'

Julia shrugged. 'We'll do what we can when we have to. And you might be surprised.'

And she was smiling a grim smile as the three of us packed away the picnic and headed for the beach.

We took the car as far as we could, to keep ourselves out of sight as much as possible. Driving slowly along the beach road, we stared out at the sea like tourists on a pilgrimage to the coast.

It was cooler by the water, especially since thin cloud had moved in to cover the sun, and a slightly chilly wind was blowing along the beach. And since the beach itself was made of big, hard pebbles rather than soft sand, we didn't see many people on it.

We also couldn't see very far, looking at the sea, since a haze had gathered offshore. As we drove on I was beginning to wonder if the haze was natural or some kind of magical veiling.

But then we went around a curve in the road, where it led on to bare open land out of sight of any villages.

And there we saw it.

At first it looked like a shapeless smudge on the surface of the water, quite a way from shore. But as the wind stirred up the haze we saw it more clearly.

An island about the size of three or four football pitches, flat and greyish-brown and empty except for patches of coarse grass and scrub brush. No trees, no hillocks, not much of anything except blank mud and sand.

'If that's the Cartel base,' Bertrand muttered, 'it's *very* well hidden.'

'As you'd expect,' Julia said.

I ignored the small chill down my spine and gathered myself. 'Let's go down to the water,' I said. 'Have a good look.'

Bertrand nodded, but Julia held back. 'I'll stay in the car,' she said. 'They'll know there are three of us, and they could be watching for a threesome.'

That made sense, so Bertrand and I set off. But first I took the sheathed knife off my belt, put it into my inside pocket and zipped the jacket. I didn't expect to need it on a mostly empty beach, and I wanted to keep it hidden from any magical eyes that might spot it.

Then we ambled across the road, trying to appear like holidaymakers with nothing much to do and too much time to do it in.

Walking on the pebbles wasn't that easy, and I was really hoping that we wouldn't have to run for our lives on that beach. But there was no sign of any kind of threat, or even of anyone paying any attention to us.

I saw only a young couple walking away from us hand in hand, and a boy and a dog playing even further away. And, at the very edge of the water, a stooped old white-haired man in a crumpled hat, long coat and wellies stood holding a huge fishing rod. It seemed almost too much for him, its line almost invisible as it trailed far out into the waves.

We wandered past him, peering at the island, and he blinked at us curiously and gave us a friendly nod. Bertrand returned it briefly, then got back to staring at the island, as I was.

I was getting a sinking feeling that it was nothing more than a dull, boring hump of dirt. But even if it was an amazing bit of magical disguise, I couldn't think of how we could find out. Bertrand and I definitely couldn't go out there to look at it – not across salt water. And I wouldn't want Julia to go alone . . .

'Nothin' much to see there,' a voice said.

We jumped and turned. The old fisherman was watching us, grinning.

'I was wondering why the island was so empty, unused,' Bertrand said, smoothly getting into the fake-tourist role. 'It would be ideal for boating, fishing, swimming . . .'

'Not likely,' the old man said cheerfully. 'Land out

there's too mucky, lots of pools an' quicksands. Worse at high tide.' His grin widened, showing a few straggly teeth. 'Way back in the real olden days, it were part of a neck of land reachin' out to sea. You could walk all along it. But then the sea swallowed most of it, just left that island.'

'Oh, interesting,' Bertrand said, happy to keep the old man talking.

'An' it surely got *used* in the olden days, but not for boatin' or any of that.' The old man chortled. 'It were a place of *punishment*. Criminals an' traitors got took out there to be hanged. Witches got burned there.' He wheezed with merry laughter, enjoying himself. 'Nowadays people round here reckon it's haunted. One way or another, nobody goes near it.'

I scowled. If it was the secret, hidden Cartel base, tales of hauntings would be as useful as warnings of quicksand, to keep people away.

'Does it have a name?' I asked idly.

'Not official, like,' the old man said. 'But people round here had a name for it since the olden days. We call it Execution Island.'

24

That was gruesome enough by itself, I thought, to put anyone off the place. Especially idly curious tourists, as we were supposed to be. So we thanked the old man and turned away.

But he seemed to think that telling us about the grisly 'olden days' was more fun than sea-fishing. Especially since he didn't seem to be catching anything.

'There's a story,' he called after us. We turned back to him as he went on. ''Bout a man from a big university. A hunnerd years ago or so, came to see the island. All keen on the history an' that, wanted to look for anythin' left from the old hangin's. Went out in a boat.' More wheezing laughter. 'Some fishermen thought they heard screamin'. An' that history man, he was never seen again.'

Bertrand raised an eyebrow. 'It certainly does sound like a place to avoid. Anyway –' he looked back up the beach away from the island – 'we'd best be heading back.' He nodded to the old man. 'We'll leave you to your fishing . . .'

'It's quite peculiar, though, you know,' the old man added.

Oddly, his voice had changed. No longer wheezing, no more touches of a local accent. A quiet and more well-spoken voice – with a hint of sardonic laughter.

'You see,' he went on, 'in the *present* day, not only do the locals stay well away from the island. No visitors to the area pay any attention to it, if they even notice it. They certainly don't ever ask *questions* about it.' He smiled, tight-lipped. 'At least, the Powerless ones don't.'

Bertrand made a small sound like a muffled groan, and I saw that he was slumped and swaying, his eyes closed. As if something unseen had stunned him.

And before I could do anything more than curse myself for putting the knife out of easy reach, the old man twitched the hand that was holding the long fishing rod. The line leaped out of the water and wrapped itself around and around me, coil upon coil, so that my arms and legs were bound.

It looked no thicker than a shiny thread, but it held me as unbreakably as steel chains. And as I struggled helplessly, and Bertrand swayed drunkenly out of control, the old man changed.

The hat and coat and boots vanished. So did the white hair, the wrinkles, the stoop, the snaggle-teeth. In his place, still holding the fishing rod, stood a tall man in an elegant dark suit.

But he was a long way from good-looking. His hair was a tangled mass that looked a lot like slimy black seaweed. His eyes were yellowish tilted ovals. And the visible skin of his face and hands was rough and scaly and scabby, split open in many places, with a foul ooze showing in the cracks.

'Mr Doul will be pleased to be proved right,' he said. 'Everyone thought he was mad to keep insisting that you two had joined forces and would find your way here.'

His smile showed two rows of sharp yellowish teeth. 'I am Mr Gavaric, by the way. In the service of Mr Kannis. And I'm so glad you arrived while I was on watch. They want your actor friend alive – but I will now get to choose the painful manner of your death.'

I probably could have spoken, but I said nothing. Cartel sorcerers on any level like the sound of their own voice, especially when they're gleefully promising to torture and kill me. And as long as he kept talking, he probably wouldn't start doing anything worse.

But the trouble was that I wasn't likely to start doing anything at all.

The bonds that surely weren't just fishing line were immovable. And no one was going to help me. The beach was empty by then, and even if there'd been a crowd we were probably magically hidden.

From Julia too, I guessed, though there was no way I could turn to look at the car.

Still showing his teeth in a savage grin, Gavaric set the rod down and stepped closer.

'I shall probably make my masters cross,' he hissed, 'but it's hard to resist. It has been said that there is something special about the blood of the Changeless Boy. Perhaps a special essence in it – perhaps only an unusually delicious flavour. So I must sample it, before I take you to them.'

He grasped my hair and tilted my head sideways. I fought even more wildly against my bonds, but they didn't give so much as a millimetre as he leaned towards me, his ugly mouth reaching for my throat.

But he never got there.

Impossibly, the bonds that held me so tightly suddenly seemed to melt away. In the same instant, just as impossibly, the knife somehow leaped from inside my zipped-up jacket into my left hand.

My mind went blank for a moment as Gavaric's eyes bulged with shock. But though he was a monster and a sorcerer, his reflexes were slower than mine.

I drove the knife into the pit of his stomach, angling it upwards so that the blade found his heart.

He was dead before he could make a sound. As he

crumpled on to the pebbles, his body seemed to turn slightly hazy – and then just vanished.

I turned towards Bertrand, thinking it must have been him who freed me. He had fallen when Gavaric's death broke the spell that had held him, and he was still just lying there on the pebbles. Conscious, apparently unhurt, but groaning softly.

And staring, pale and wide-eyed, at something behind me.

I whirled about, knife ready. But there was no new Cartel menace. All I saw was a woman standing beside the car we'd come in.

Except – the woman wasn't Julia.

She was a bit taller, not so thin. She was wearing a longish blue dress made of some shiny material. She had huge green eyes and long thick red-gold hair.

I knew her well.

Manta.

25

I started towards her, blindly, the knife still in my hand. I had no real idea what I was doing or going to do, since my mind was a storm of tangled feelings. And uppermost in those feelings was *fury*.

This was the first time I'd seen Manta herself – not in one of the dream-visions she'd sent me – since the night, years before, when she had made me changeless. But I wasn't furious with her just because she'd hidden herself from me for so long.

I was mainly furious because I'd realized, in a flash, *where* she'd been hiding.

Running over those loose pebbles was just as hard as I'd thought, but I plunged on towards her – and was surprised to find Bertrand stumbling along just behind me. And Manta stood motionless, waiting for us.

'You're much better with the knife than you were the first time, Nick,' she said, a smile curving her red lips.

'Manta!' Bertrand cried. 'You're *alive*! Where have you *been*?'

And for some reason that made me even angrier. 'Wake *up*!' I yelled at Bertrand. 'Don't you see? *She's been Julia!*'

Bertrand staggered as if I'd hit him. And as we lurched from the beach, across the street towards the car, Manta seemed to shimmer and grow hazy.

And we were looking at thin, blonde Julia again.

'Quick as ever,' she said to me, still smiling. And she might have said more, but my anger burst out.

'Why did you *do* it?' I raged. 'Why did you *pretend*, all this time? *Why didn't you ever TELL me?*'

Her pale eyes flashed. 'I've let you know now, so that I could save both your lives. You might consider that. And I'll tell you the rest of it, if you wish. But first we have to get away from here.'

She turned quickly towards the car, and we followed – Bertrand still wide-eyed, me still fuming. Some bit of sense in my mind tried to tell me that I wasn't being very reasonable. But then I never was, on the subject of Manta.

I'd been angry with her for a long time. For putting the curse of Changelessness on me, which set the Cartel on my trail. For her vague, annoying dream-messages that were never much use. For staying in hiding, never using her great power to help me.

Or, especially, to help April . . .

So the storm went on in my mind as the car roared

away, leaving the shore and the island behind. And no one said a word until we came to a stop on the side of a back road surrounded by flat farmland, where nothing looked threatening all the way to the horizon.

Both Bertrand and I then started at once, but her raised hand stopped us. 'Let me tell you,' she said, 'rather than have you question me and shout at me.'

So she began.

'I was fighting the Cartel, doing them a lot of damage,' she said. 'And not long after we first met, Nick, they began going all out to find me – their psychics, every kind of seeking spell, all of it. They started getting too close, too often, and it seemed only a matter of time before they finished me. So I decided to disappear. By becoming Julia.'

'Without telling anyone,' I said through my teeth.

'More or less,' she said. 'The Cartel has many horrible ways to make people reveal secrets – as you know, Nick.'

That stopped me. I remembered how the Cartel wanted to use me, when I was their prisoner, to track Manta through the dream-visions she sent me. Which of course would explain why she stopped sending them . . .

'Didn't you even tell Paddy?' I snarled.

She sighed. 'Paddy and I go back a long way. We first met when I was quite young, when I was studying with his uncle, Alderon. But then we went different ways, and soon I foolishly married Bertrand.'

'Oh, come—' Bertrand began.

Her fierce glance silenced him. 'Years later I found Paddy again, and we . . . got together. And when I decided to hide, to become Julia, Paddy *insisted* that I put a spell on him – so that he would be unable to reveal my secret, no matter what was done to him.' She gave me a sad look. 'I would have done the same for you, Nick. But Paddy convinced me that you would be safer if you simply didn't know where Manta had gone. Which the Cartel would realize.'

'I've never been *safe*!' I yelled. 'Not since I met you!'

Her mouth tightened. 'Are we going through all that again? How I committed such a *crime* against you, by making you as you are? I'll say to you what you said to Bertrand – *wake up*, Nick! Without me you would have stayed on those bitter unforgiving streets, half starved and half alive, waiting for some accident or disease or moment of violence to finish you off. I *transformed* you! You're a warrior now, with many victories to your name! You're a *legend*, Nick – the Changeless Boy whose presence makes even top-level mages like Doul look nervously over their shoulder!'

'Makes them keen to kill me, more like,' I snapped.

'Everyone dies, Nick,' she said flatly. 'But when it's your turn, you won't be snivelling in a dirty gutter.

You'll be fighting as ever against our evil enemies. Which is a much better way to go.'

'She's not wrong, old chap,' Bertrand muttered.

I wasn't so sure of that, but I could see I wasn't going to win that argument. 'But while I was out there fighting for my life against the demon stalkers,' I said to her, 'where were *you*? Safely hidden away, not caring—'

'I *did* care!' she cried. 'But much of the time I was fighting my own battles against the horrors they sent after me. And after I got together with Paddy and became Julia, I briefly lost touch with you. I can do no magic in Julia's Powerless form. But now and then I risked becoming Manta again, for a few moments, to search for you magically. And when I located you that summer, Paddy went to find you and bring you home to us.'

That shut me up. I'd always thought my meeting Paddy was purely good luck, the second happiest accident of my life. Then I thought of the first happiest, and the realization made me shocked all over again.

Julia – Manta – probably also had something to do with my finding April. She must have located April somehow, and aimed me towards the series of events that led to her wild rescue. But if Julia/Manta had done that, it meant that what I'd suspected for months was true.

'So you set me up to rescue April too,' I muttered.

'Exactly,' she said. 'And you might remember that, when you next feel like raging at me. Because of me you met Paddy, who became your friend. Through me you met April, who I think you care about deeply. Thanks to me, Nick, you're no longer *alone*!'

I took a deep breath, as the truth of that struck home. And the part of my mind that was telling me to be reasonable said something like '*See?*'

Bertrand was frowning. 'But *why* did you send Nick to find April?'

We both glared at his dimness. 'April's her *daughter*,' I said.

Julia's blue eyes filled with tears. 'And I wasn't able to protect her . . .'

'Daughter?' Bertrand cried. 'Really! I did think, when I saw her on the Path, that she looked familiar somehow! Her mouth, the shape of her face . . . And is Paddy the father?'

Then he flinched, because Julia/Manta was giving him a fierce look again. 'When she was not quite three and was stolen by the Cartel for the first time, it was *long* before I found Paddy again. In fact, she was born not long after you left me, *Bertie*, for that fluffy little actress. It was all very sudden, you'll remember, so I never got to tell you that I was pregnant. It wasn't her resemblance to *me* that looked familiar, you fool. She looks a lot like her father – especially the eyes.'

I looked at Bertrand, and saw it. The bright, clear hazel eyes – though April's were bigger and brighter . . .

'You mean *I'm* her father . . .?' Bertrand croaked, looking stunned again.

'You are.' She leaned towards him, glaring. 'And that's why you'll stay with us – that's why you'll help us, and fight at our side. Because whoever and whatever is lurking somewhere around that ugly island, *they have our daughter*!'

26

We went on sitting there a while, and Bertrand went on looking fairly stunned, while Julia explained herself a bit more. She told me how she'd got Paddy to try to talk me out of my early notion that April was her daughter because of the risk of tipping off the Cartel.

'I lived in constant fear that they would discover me,' she said. 'Through my – Julia's – link with you, Nick, and with April. A top sorcerer like Redman or Kannis might well have broken through my disguise.' Her mouth twitched in a sour half-smile. 'But to them I was just a poor, timid, Powerless woman, and they didn't even look at me.'

She also told us how she had nearly revealed herself as Manta several times – despite the terrible risk, with the Cartel seeking her – when things got desperate. Like the time when the Skryl demon found me and I fled to draw it away from them. Or especially the time when the Cartel invaded their house, after I'd gone, to recapture April – but struck her down before she could change her form.

She'd also intended to become Manta when they came to Redman's house to help April and me, but again Redman struck too quickly. And she would have become Manta to get us into Doul's house, after we'd seen April there – but finding Bertrand meant she didn't have to.

'So you let me take the risks,' Bertrand complained. 'How kind. And of course you let Nick and me do the fighting, since I suppose you still can't kill anyone or even spill blood.'

'Correct,' she said calmly. 'It's because of my book,' she told me, seeing my frown. 'The Book of the Craft – unlike any other – which I discovered while I was with Alderon. To prevent itself from being used for evil, it forbids murder or blood-spilling. I'd lose all my powers if I broke that law.'

'So we get to do your dirty work,' Bertrand muttered.

'It's our work too,' I said. By then I was starting to listen to that small, sensible part of my mind, and seeing a lot of things more clearly. 'And anyway, we'd be back on that beach right now, in big trouble or dead, if it wasn't for her.' I turned to look at her. 'I'm sorry I lost it just now,' I told her. 'I can only imagine what we might be facing if we keep going, and so, I guess, I'm glad you're here.'

She reached out to lay her hand on mine. 'Apology accepted –' she smiled gently at me – '. . . my son.'

'*Son?*' Bertrand gasped, looking shocked.

'In a way,' Manta said kindly. 'After all, I *am* the creator of the Changeless Boy.'

And then we were all smiling, and the mood was ridiculously light-hearted as she started the car and we drove away.

We needed to find a place to stay, since that eventful day was coming to an end. None of us was too happy about being anywhere near the island after dark, but it didn't really matter.

We'd surely alerted the enemy by putting down the scabby sorcerer on the beach. I knew there probably wasn't any place, night or day, near the island or across the country, where we could feel safe.

All we could do was be ready for them, if they came. So we found a guest house on a main street of the village where we'd been earlier, and took a family room at the front on the second floor – the top floor – for the three of us.

That seemed to fluster Bertrand a little, which might have been funny under different circumstances. After making another small inroad into our food, for a supper that no one much wanted, we settled in and watched the twilight gather.

We didn't talk much. It didn't seem that Manta and Bertrand had a lot to say to each other, and she wasn't likely to start telling stories of her long lone battle against the Cartel. Nor was I.

My head was still spinning a little, still amazed that after all those years Manta was there with me in that drab room, and would be with me during the *next* battle against the enemy.

And I remembered what I'd said to myself when I'd first set out on that hopeless quest with the person I'd thought was Julia. *Do them as much damage as possible*, I'd thought, *before we fall.*

But now I'd be tackling them in company with the fairly powerful magic of Bertrand and the greater, more complex power of Manta.

We'll be doing more damage than I ever imagined, I thought. And if we could somehow get to April, the real April, and set *her* free . . .

Such, almost hopeful, thoughts were still swarming in my mind when full darkness had spread across the village. But I managed at last to fall asleep, with Manta – in her real form, ready to use her magic – taking the first shift on guard.

I didn't wake up when Bertrand took over. But I was wide awake, feeling quite refreshed and ready, when it was my turn, well after midnight. I moved a chair over beside the window and sat there, listening, the knife drawn and ready by my side.

It was hard, but not impossible, to stop myself imagining what Cartel horror might come crashing in at me. But what did come through the window a few moments later was something I'd never expected.

A soft, light voice calling my name.

April's voice.

'Nick, can you hear me?' she called. 'They're *after* me, Nick! *Help* me!'

27

I moved closer to the window, cupping my hands around the knife-blade to muffle its glow, peering out.

She was standing on the pavement below, staring up at me. The street was totally deserted, as far as I could see. A street-light further along showed her pale face turned up to me. She looked much as she had at Doul's house, but in another dress – and, more importantly, as far as I could see in that light, her face was different.

Not the blank, empty expression of the soulless body. It looked like *April.*

A murmur behind me told me that my movement had brought Manta awake – if she'd been sleeping – and she was waking Bertrand. They joined me, peering down.

'Please, *hurry*!' April called. 'They're looking for me!'

I felt desperate and wary and urgent, all at the same time. But Bertrand put his hand on my arm. 'It could be a trap,' he muttered.

'Maybe not,' I said. 'That looks like the real April.'

'She might have been reunited with her soul,' Manta whispered, 'and managed to escape . . .'

That was enough for me. I pulled my arm away from Bertrand's hand, sheathed the knife, flung the window open and went straight out of it.

I hadn't gone crazy, jumping from a second-floor window. The guest house's front garden had several good-sized trees, and one was close enough. I did a slightly clumsy monkey act – leaping as far as I could from the windowsill, crashing into the branches, half falling and half climbing down through them to land with a thump on the lawn.

April had moved into the garden as I leaped, standing by the shadow of thick shrubs, smiling shakily at me. Then I flinched, startled, when Bertrand magically appeared beside me, a lot more gracefully.

'April!' I gasped. 'Who's after you? Where are they?'

'Oh, Nick,' she said, 'it's so good to see you . . .' But as she reached towards me, her smile twisted, and she laughed in a voice that wasn't hers.

And two shadows beneath the shrubs loomed towards us, revealing themselves as monsters.

They both seemed to be made of stone, but not like smooth statues. Their huge hulking bodies were *carved*, all angled facets and corners like cut glass or jewels.

They were both the same size and the same dark red colour, and both had small greenish eyes glinting from under heavy brows.

As I stared, the being that looked like April moved a hand in a magical gesture and Bertrand gave a small sigh and went stiff. Then she changed form – becoming a tall, thin, leggy woman in shiny-black tights and leotard, like a circus tumbler.

Except that she was completely hairless. Her pale skin had green veins all over it, and her eyes were huge and slanted and as colourless as cold rain.

'I am Ms Harmal.' Her voice was thin, slightly shrill. 'And it's so nice of you to come down to greet me.'

As she laughed again, an eerie giggle, and raised her hand towards me, I felt a faint tug at my belt. But before I could move, invisible wrappings formed around my upper body, binding my arms in a way that I was getting to know all too well.

Struggling uselessly, I glanced down and saw to my shock that the sheathed knife had vanished from my belt. But I could see that the weird woman didn't have it, and nor did the monsters . . .

Manta, I thought. For some reason, she wasn't willing to fight this woman and her monsters, but didn't want the knife to be lost to them either . . .

Then I stopped thinking about that, because the evil hairless woman, still giggling, had beckoned the two giant monsters closer. And the light from the street showed that they weren't twins after all.

Their faces had been carved more carefully, and though they were oversized and distorted, I recognized them. And nearly screamed.

One face was made to look like Paddy, the other like Sam Foss.

'Are you glad to see your friends?' The woman's giggle was like chalk squeaking on slate. 'Their souls are held in these crystal shapes, although they cannot *control* their new bodies . . .'

She didn't seem to be able to control her cruel giggling either, as I began struggling wildly against the invisible bonds, raging at her. By then Bertrand seemed awake again, also struggling against the sorcery that bound him and his magic. And I had the feeling that the woman's laughter was sounding a little strained. In fact she was *looking* a little strained.

As if the magic she was doing was pushing her to her limits.

Not a high-level sorcerer then, I thought. Maybe on the same level in the Cartel as the three who served Fray at Redman's house. Which was sort of encouraging. I wondered if Manta knew that this veiny witch wasn't extra powerful.

More importantly, I wondered where Manta *was*.

Eerily, the woman answered the question as if I'd

spoken it. Tilting her head, she peered up at our window as if listening, then shrugged.

'Your Powerless woman friend has fled in terror, poor thing,' she said, smiling. 'But no matter. She can be tracked and gathered up after we have got you two safely to the castle.'

Castle? Where would that be? I wondered. But at least Manta had got away, in her Julia disguise. With the knife. That was encouraging too.

The woman stepped closer, looking me up and down. 'You're said to carry a special weapon – a knife?'

I thought fast. 'I . . . It was taken from me. At Doul's.'

Her thin lips twitched. 'So Mr Doul has claimed it. Too bad. I had hoped to have it myself.'

'You might get it yet,' I snarled. 'The blade anyway. In your throat.'

That brought another giggle, as she waved a hand. And the two monsters picked up Bertrand and me as if we weighed nothing and followed the woman as she stalked towards the street.

She was heading for a big ordinary camper van parked on the other side of the street. Not using magic, I realized, to get us wherever we were going. Definitely not high-level.

The silent monsters dumped Bertrand and me into the van through the sliding side door, then climbed in after us, never taking their little green eyes off us. And the woman, Harmal, went round to the driver's door and got behind the wheel.

'It won't be long now,' she told me. 'And then you'll have all your questions answered, about the place that the Powerless call Execution Island.' Another snigger. 'Just think – you'll be the very latest in a long line of miserable wretches taken there to die.'

28

She drove in a stiff, jerky way, rather like the way she walked, but the streets were mostly empty. And anyway, I didn't pay much attention. I was too busy trying to stay calm in the face of the shattering fact that all our attempts to hide and stay watchful had been useless.

I was a prisoner of the Cartel again. Along with April, as before. And Paddy and Sam and Bertrand. We probably wouldn't be flung back to the Downward Path this time. But that did nothing for my state of mind.

We were almost certainly being taken, instead, to the Cartel's secret base, to be faced with the demonic Kannis and the soul-twisting horror of the Head.

And I knew that the shock of it all, including the misery of seeing what had happened to Paddy and Sam, would be only the first in a series of new torments and terrors ahead of me.

The ironic thing was that she was actually taking me exactly where I'd wanted to go. I'd just hoped to get there under my own steam. Still, the thought of being in the same place as April and, it seemed likely, Paddy and Sam too, provided me with a small glimmer of hope. I'd been a prisoner before and lived to tell the tale. But then . . . things got worse.

Harmal halted the van on the empty road that ran along the beach, and I stared out of the side window at the flat, dark mass of the island, just visible out on the faintly glimmering water.

Then she giggled, and spoke a single ugly word. Which let me see the island as it truly was.

A wide causeway stretched out to it from the shore – a mass of dark shiny stone that I realized would rest solidly on the seabed. Not a bridge but an artificial solidity that made the island, once again, merely the end of a peninsula. A *headland*, as Bertrand had joked – even less funny now.

It would normally be invisible, of course, but not to the Cartel. So magical people could get to the island without going over salt water.

And Harmal's magic also showed me what they – and we – would be going *to*.

Definitely a castle, but from a horror film, not a fairy tale. Built of inky black stone that glittered slightly, it rose many storeys high, covered in narrow balconies and gables and other decorations, including some gruesome gargoyles. At the sides, two tall squared-off towers rose even higher, with a sweep of battlements on the roof between them, like a giant row of black teeth.

A lot of windows glowed yellow from those dark walls, and a few more lit up as Harmal sent the van jouncing over the beach, then smoothly across the causeway.

The enormous front door, mostly dark metal, was firmly shut – but she swung around to the side, where another door stood open, light spilling out.

'See, you're expected,' she said. 'And I promise you'll be welcome. So much so that no one will ever want you to leave!'

That really creased her up. But as she giggled, and as the two monsters took hold of Bertrand and me, I felt another touch.

Totally unexpected, totally amazing, so that I needed every bit of self-control to keep myself from reacting. A light gentle touch – like a woman's cool hand resting for an instant on my cheek.

So I was smiling to myself as we were carried in through the door. Manta had been in the van with us, unseen. She was on the island, safe and free, and no one knew it but me.

Still, her presence gave me only a glimmer of hope. I couldn't imagine what she could do for any of us, all by herself against such opposition.

And that glimmer of hope shrank and all but disappeared when I saw what was waiting inside.

Harmal and the two monsters dragged us into a fairly ordinary entrance hall, with a pale stone floor and a number of passages leading from it in different directions. In the centre of the open space stood ten or twelve beings who weren't at all ordinary. Or human.

They looked like insects, something like ants, and they were clearly some kind of guards, or what Cartel sorcerers liked to call 'watchmen'. They were all quite a bit taller than me, standing upright on two legs so that the four others became arms. The legs and arms and necks were very skinny, but that didn't mean much. I'd read something once about how incredibly strong ants were, for their size.

Their long, lumpy bodies were covered in thick, dark, shiny shell, like armour, and the same shell covered their huge heads like helmets, except for the thin antennae, large round blank eyes and pinched lipless mouths.

Worst of all, their forelegs ended in narrow hands with four fingers tapering to claws like blades, and each of them gripped a short heavy spear with a long, barbed and deadly sharp blade.

But they were only part of the welcoming committee.

In front of the insect group stood something a lot

more frightening. Something tall, thin, all in white, with narrow, inhuman eyes as stony-black as a vampire's heart.

The sorcerer Doul, whom I clearly hadn't killed, and who would have been healed by Cartel magic. Staring at me with the kind of malevolent, vengeful hatred I'd had from Fray, but maybe worse.

'You must be more foolish than I thought,' he snarled, 'if you thought you could elude us and be safe coming here. And for all your lucky escapes from our hunters in the past, here now your luck will end.' His thin smile held no humour, only cruel rage and bitter spite. 'You face a prolonged time of unbelievable agony, which I shall personally oversee – while your feeble play-actor friend will walk the Path again until we alter his nature and make him ours. And when we grow bored with you, boy, the Head himself will do you the honour of finishing you . . .' He paused. 'But I must not spoil the surprise of that.'

I was working on keeping still, holding my head up, staring into his horrible eyes and showing nothing. I also managed to keep my voice steady.

'He won't have the chance,' I said, 'if you talk me to death.'

The black eyes flared and he started towards me, hands lifting, fingers curling like bony claws. As I braced myself, and the insect-watchmen stirred, Doul managed to find enough control to stop himself.

'Take them away,' he ordered, his voice shaking a little with fury. 'If they find a way to try to resist, restrain them. But do not kill them. *Months* of anguish await them, especially the boy, before that release.'

29

So we were dragged away by the watchmen, led by Harmal through a shadowy maze of high-ceilinged corridors and hallways. In the dim light I could see that it was all fairly well looked after, no dust or cracked plaster. But even so, the whole place smelt stale and musty, as if windows were never opened. And it was chilly and a bit clammy, even though it was summer.

Bertrand still looked half stunned, as if Harmal's spell was muffling his mind as well as his magic. But I was trying to stay alert and calm, trying to memorize our route from the outer door we'd come through. After all, I told myself firmly, we'd need to know how to get out when Manta came to help us escape.

Which, I needed to tell myself, she would do.

I fixed the route in my mind in terms of the decorations here and there along those passageways – tall vases, small carved tables, tapestries, a lot of paintings. Most of the images were fairly ugly and disturbing, none more than a portrait of a scrawny old woman who was the ugliest hag I'd ever seen.

She wore a rich heavy gown in the picture, and a lot of jewellery, but it didn't help. Her white hair was straggly and wild, her hands were bony and clawed, her thin, twisted mouth showed a glimpse of pointed fangs. Worse, her face seemed to be streaked with patches of lurid blue, and her eyes were scarlet slits.

Her image was glaring straight out of the portrait – and, as often happens, those red eyes seemed to follow me as we went by. It was creepy, and I must have shown how I felt.

'Amazing, isn't she?' Harmal said. 'You may know that this castle originally belonged to Mr Kannis's family. It was translocated here, to the island, to be the nerve centre of the Cartel after the Head first came to form it. And that lady in the picture, the greatest witch of her time, is Mr Kannis's great-grandmother.'

It was hard to imagine Kannis being young and having a granny. And I didn't want to let myself think what the rest of the family looked like.

We hadn't been on the move for too long when we came to an open door at the end of a side passage. The door glinted, because it was made of metal – and so was the small room beyond it. A totally bare room, no windows, just a hard, shiny metal box.

'Have a little rest,' Harmal said, grinning, as the

watchmen set us down on the metal floor and filed out. 'Your agonies will begin before long.'

As she went out, the unseen bonds fell away from us, and Bertrand jumped when the door clanged tightly shut.

So tight that I couldn't even see the seams around it.

We stayed like that, trapped in a metal box, for two days without anything at all happening to us. I'd never owned a watch, but I'd learned to estimate the passing of time quite accurately. Even when it passed as painfully slowly as it did then.

The room had some of the same magic that we found on the Downward Path, so that we didn't need to sleep or eat or use a toilet. So we didn't even have those little breaks from the unbelievable monotony of sitting or standing or lying on a blank metal floor staring at a blank metal wall.

We talked a bit, of course, but just chit-chat. We both knew it was likely that a Cartel psychic would be listening in. Psychics can't really read minds, but they can sometimes pick up hints of thoughts when they're clearly formed into spoken words. So we were careful.

Especially when we mentioned a certain person who'd been with us before.

'It's good that, ah, Julia got away,' Bertrand had said, soon after Harmal had closed the door.

'Yeah,' I said. 'Lucky.'

'Wonder where she's got to,' Bertrand said, doing a good job of sounding idly curious.

I waved a hand in a circular motion. 'She'll be around. Somewhere.'

At that Bertrand gave me a small fierce grin and changed the subject.

But after those two achingly long empty days, we'd run out of things to talk about and any interest in talking at all. Bertrand had offered to help pass the time by reciting some of the great speeches from Shakespeare's plays, but I preferred to be left in silence, to lose myself in daydreams.

Dreams about finding a way to make a heroic escape, rescuing April and everyone. Or about April appearing as she was on Fray's eerie landscape before the Head came. When she'd been a dazzling angel in golden armour, ablaze with fury, facing Kannis himself and matching his power . . .

Or a slightly more likely dream of Manta finding her way to us and making something happen.

But in those two days there had been no hint of her. Maybe, I thought, because the magic of that room was somehow blocking her powers.

I usually managed to stop myself from thinking that they'd discovered her and she too was a prisoner. Or dead.

'It must be one of their tortures, leaving us like this,' Bertrand said, jolting me out of a daydream about April and Manta, side by side, blasting the castle to ruins.

'I've been tortured by the Cartel,' I muttered. 'This is better.'

'Maybe something has happened,' Bertrand said. 'Something that's keeping them all busy, so they've forgotten us.'

I shrugged. Talking about 'maybe' was another sort of daydream, not good for much except passing the time . . .

Then I gasped and sat up straight.

Someone had spoken my name.

As Bertrand stared I started to whirl to see who it was. But then I realized that I hadn't *heard* the voice in the usual way.

It had spoken inside my mind. A soft whisper, sounding like Manta.

But it wasn't.

'Nick,' the voice whispered again, 'it's me, April.'

30

So I learned, to my delight, that Kannis and company had a real problem. It was April's spirit or soul that was talking to me, still outside the blank obedient body we met at Doul's. But her spirit wasn't a prisoner in some other grisly form.

She had *escaped*. Her spirit was roaming free within the castle.

'I could have got out,' she told me, 'but I have to find a way to get my body back and help Paddy and Sam. And I would have sent you a message long ago, but you were moving around the country a lot, and anyway they might have spotted it. But I knew you were trying to find me. And I'm *so* glad you're here, though I'm sorry you got caught.'

At least she had her magical powers in that form, she said. Not at full output, she thought, but they were there. So while the Cartel sorcerers were frantically searching for her, she could keep her spirit-self hidden.

Right then, in fact, she was hiding in the portrait of

the old horror-witch, Kannis's great-granny. Its eyes really *had* been following me, because they were April's.

She was taking the risk of speaking to me, she said, because the Head had come back. She didn't know why he sometimes left or where he went, but she knew when he was there. And Kannis and Doul and Harmal were wrapped up in some kind of meeting with him, probably sorting out a lot of other Cartel business besides what was going on in the castle.

So it was a bit safer, then, for April to use magic. And she was speaking to me on a sort of psychic tight beam, which other psychics wouldn't easily pick up. I could even reply, if I kept my focus and *spoke* in my mind in clear words and images.

I suppose there was a lot that both of us wanted to say to each other, but we mostly talked about what we – she – might do. The problem was that she felt she'd be overmatched, facing the Head, Kannis, Doul and Harmal all together. It was a bit of a help when I killed Gavaric, but not enough.

'I don't dare use my magic for anything big,' she said sadly, 'which would lead them to me. That means I can't try to get you out of that cell.'

'Nowhere to go, anyway,' I said.

'There's also Paddy and Sam to think about,' she said. 'And something else. I've sensed a new presence in the castle – female and magical. Keeping herself hidden too, so she can't be Cartel . . .'

I formed the images in my head as best I could, and April's inner voice nearly shrieked. 'It's *Manta*? And she was *Julia* all along? Oh, Nick – if she's as powerful as you've always said – and if you and Bertrand could somehow get out of there – we might have a *chance*!'

But I remembered how, in Fray's desert, the Head had so easily extinguished the power of both April and Sam and carried them off. Even Manta wasn't going to improve our chances, I thought gloomily, against the combined power of the Head plus three of his sorcerers.

Anyway, unless April managed some sort of magic to smash down our cell's metal door without revealing herself in the process, I knew there was no way Bertrand and I were going to get out.

But of course there was. We could be *taken* out.

And April's voice vanished from my mind when the door was flung open.

'Having fun, boys?' Harmal sneered, with the Paddy and Sam monsters looming behind her and a squad of insect-watchmen behind them.

'It's been very peaceful,' Bertrand said icily.

'Wish you could have joined us,' I said through my teeth.

'Never mind – now it gets exciting,' she grinned. 'The Head of the Cartel wants to take a look at you.'

So we were marched away again, through the mazy corridors. We didn't pass the horrible portrait where April's spirit was hiding, and she'd broken off contact when Harmal arrived. But not everyone had.

As we paused in front of a huge double door that an elephant could have gone through with room to spare, I felt that light cool touch again. Manta's invisible hand gripping mine and squeezing.

I had no idea how she managed to stay unseen in that nest of evil sorcerers and psychics, but I was desperately glad that she could, and that she was still alive.

So I was wearing a small smile as the doors opened and Harmal led us through.

But then terror wiped my smile off.

We had entered an immense room, its ceiling only dimly visible in the murky shadows high above me. The stone floor was polished and gleaming, the walls were draped in colourful tapestries. On the far side, two wide steps went up on to a higher level, where the floor was covered by a rich, soft colourful carpet.

Slightly above the carpet, the giant monstrosity of the Head floated motionlessly.

It – he – looked the same as before. The deathly grey

skin creased and blotchy, thick tangled white hair and beard, vast mouth with thick rubbery black lips and terrifying eyes the colour of lava, with shiny facets like huge rubies.

The red eyes were fixed on Kannis, elegantly suited and devil-faced as ever, standing beside the Head, talking with what looked like urgency, but too far away for me to hear. But he stopped when the Head growled like distant thunder, licking his lips with a slimy black tongue.

'If you cannot deal with it without going there, leave it for now.' The huge voice wasn't bellowing as it had been when the Head appeared in the sky to end the fight that Fray had started, but it was still loud enough to make the floor quiver slightly. 'I need all of you here, until our problem has been solved.'

Kannis shrugged and nodded, saying something else I couldn't hear.

'I am well aware of it,' the Head boomed in reply. 'But the girl will provide the solution to many problems, when we have overcome her. You and Doul may feel hampered without a third senior mage, but Harmal is still young, and there are no other obvious candidates. I did have hopes of Gavaric, but . . .'

He fell silent, and the two of them turned to stare at me, as if they'd just noticed our arrival.

'And this is the one? This inconsequential child?

Who has somehow been at the heart of so many of our difficulties?' The Head's voice swelled with sudden anger. 'We DESERVE to be troubled when we have proved so UNABLE to rid ourselves of such a trivial PEST . . .'

He probably would have gone on, and got louder, with veins bulging under his pasty skin and the crimson eyes flaring. But he was distracted, by the opening of a side door.

Through it came the small, pudgy blonde teenager I'd seen at Doul's house – his junior sorcerer, Stoll. Behind her an insect-watchman stalked, one clawed hand gripping the arm of another creature.

This new one looked mostly human, and unthreatening – child-sized and naked.

But its soft, pale doughy body had no genitals, while its smooth head and chubby face had no mouth or ears or hair. And its round eyes were as blank and empty as a marble statue's.

The anger faded from the Head's eyes. 'Is this one from the same batch? The last one was excellent.'

Stoll flinched and half bowed, clumsily. 'It is, master.'

As she spoke, the watchman led the small bare figure up the steps, towards the monstrosity, who made a noise like a growling purr. Knowing that something horrible was about to happen, I felt sudden sickness burn my throat.

It was worse than I expected.

With all the Cartel people watching calmly, as if it was a normal everyday process, the Head's magic lifted the little being into the air and moved it towards his face.

Then he opened that ghastly mouth, showing huge, flat, shiny-black teeth like long spearheads. And he bit off the little one's head and began to chew.

31

As one of the watchmen carried off the small headless body, gurgling to itself, I must have looked like I was about to throw up. Harmal was grinning evilly at me, but she didn't have time to say anything.

'Right,' Kannis snapped, coming down towards us while the Head finished his grisly snack. 'Stoll, you take these two along to Mr Doul. When Ms Harmal releases them, put your own binding spell on them. And be sure to make it strong. Nowell might be too much for you if he were free. Harmal, come with me.'

Suddenly Bertrand and I were out of the huge chamber, standing in the empty corridor – and for a fraction of an instant our arms were free. But Stoll and three watchmen were there with us, though not the two crystal monsters. And before we could move Stoll lifted a small hand, and the magical bonds reappeared around us.

'Come along, then,' Stoll said, looking a bit tense,

sounding a bit edgy. And we set off on another trek through the castle.

'Is that what the Head always eats?' I asked. I wasn't really that curious, but I hoped to wind up her tension even more and see what happened.

'I think so,' Stoll said. 'When he's here in the castle, anyway.'

Instead of growing more edgy, Stoll seemed glad of a chance to talk. Maybe she felt lonely in that place, with the older higher-level mages. The insect-watchmen didn't seem to speak at all, let alone get chatty. And I was a lot closer to her age than anyone else around.

'Does he go somewhere else, then?' I asked, remembering what Alderon had told us about his links to another ghastly dimension.

'His real home is in another realm,' Stoll said, sounding awed. 'He's a *demon lord*, you know. And the great Head isn't really *him*, it's just what he chooses to look like when he's here. No one except Mr Kannis and Mr Doul knows what he *really* looks like, or what his *name* is.'

'Naturally he'd keep his name secret,' Bertrand said, joining the conversation, his voice sounding extra warm and kindly. 'We both know about the power that lies in demon names.'

'Oh, yes,' Stoll breathed, responding like a dog being patted. 'But *all* his power is just . . . incredible.'

'I can believe that,' Bertrand murmured. 'And yet he and Mr Kannis seemed to be talking about some *problems* they were facing . . .?'

'Did they?' Stoll blinked. 'I suppose there are always problems. The Cartel has things going on here and there, different *projects*, you know . . . And I've heard them talking about some trouble that's come up with something big they're doing over in the west country . . .'

That straightened me up. 'Trouble', for one of the Cartel's vile enterprises, could mean somebody trying to wreck it. Some enemy of the Cartel. Clearly it wasn't me or Manta doing it, and I'd never heard of anyone else actively fighting the Cartel.

But there was one possibility. A very cheering one.

Perhaps because of our visit, *Alderon* might have decided to take some action – while he still could – against the evil that was his enemy too.

If you're having a go at them, Alderon, I said silently, hit them hard.

At that moment Stoll and the insects were taking us through a sort of ante-room, with a few chairs and tables but not much else, dimly lit and silent. And it almost seemed as if my silent plea about hitting the Cartel sparked what happened next.

Manta appeared out of nowhere, in front of us, with

her heavy old Book of the Craft in her hands and slammed Stoll over the head with it.

Aside from looking grim and determined, Manta looked amazing – in a kind of catsuit thing, shiny and figure-hugging – ready for action.

And just as well.

The three watchmen had frozen for half an instant as Stoll fell. Then they leaped, lunging at us with their spears.

But by then Manta had flicked the big book open, glanced at it and gasped a few words. And the bonds that Stoll had made vanished from around Bertrand and me, just in time.

The watchmen had been told to keep us alive, so they seemed to be aiming for our legs. But Bertrand's magic deflected two of them, so that they neatly drove their spears into each other and fell with a clatter.

And as I leaped high to avoid the third spear, the glowing golden-bladed knife suddenly appeared in my hand.

I was half dazed with astonishment, but my reactions weren't. Pivoting, I swung a backhand and sliced – so easily it was a bit sickening – through the third watchman's scrawny neck. As he fell, I noticed how all three bodies stayed where they were. We were definitely on Cartel home ground. In the Powerless realm dead Cartel creatures withered and vanished.

For a moment I stood over Stoll's unconscious body, knife raised. But even though I knew it was probably a mistake, I couldn't do it. Just as I hadn't been able to kill Fray, once, in cold blood. And Stoll was just a kid . . .

I glanced at Bertrand, but he shook his head and shrugged, clearly feeling just as unable to finish the girl off.

'Leave her!' Manta snapped. 'I found a place where we can hide for a while . . .'

'We can't *hide* in this place!' Bertrand gasped, looking shocked. 'We have to get *away*!'

'I've been hiding ever since you got here!' Manta spat, rage turning her eyes to emerald flame so that Bertrand took a step back. '"This place" is where we have to be, where Nick and I have been heading all along – which is why I stayed hidden when that Harmal creature took you captive! We're not going anywhere till we find our loved ones! And if you try to run out on us again, *Bertie*, I'll skin you alive!'

'And I'll help,' I snarled.

Manta whirled away towards what looked like some stairs just ahead. Bertrand glanced warily at me, sighed, and we both followed her.

'I feel a lot better now I've got my knife back.

Thanks.' I said to Manta. 'And I've got some good news for you. I've been in touch with April. The *real* April, her soul. She's free, in the castle, and I know where to find her.'

Total joy lit up Manta's face as she glanced back at me. And I was feeling weirdly cheerful as we raced away.

32

I'd seen enough of the castle to know how big it was, so it was no surprise when we saw no one else along that corridor or on the stairs. They were narrow, plain stone steps, spiralling down.

But if Kannis had servants or servitors or whatever, I hadn't seen any. And I definitely didn't think that the little bare creature so horribly killed by the Head had been a servant. It had just been food.

In fact, the Head's odd mention of a 'batch' made it sound as if the little one, and maybe others like it, might have been specially made, magically or otherwise.

I wondered if Kannis and Doul ate them too, then pushed the revolting thought away. That would be a new and grislier depth even for the Cartel. But it could be that the headless bodies went to feed the watchmen. I remembered the one who took the newly killed one away earlier. Its gurgling noise had sounded *hungry*.

The old pantry that was Manta's hiding place

probably also dated from when the castle had servants working for people who ate real food. It was windowless and dark, and when Manta made a small hovering light I saw that the place was dusty as well, and totally empty except for a few frightened bugs and hopeful spiders.

Manta was looking at her book again, muttering. Then it vanished as she looked up. 'I've wiped any trail we might have left that a mage might sense,' she said. 'If we're lucky, we might stay hidden long enough to make them think we've fled the castle. And when we move from here, Bertie, you and I can link up and do a really good veiling spell.'

'I wish you'd call me Bertrand,' he muttered. 'And whatever we do, the Head will probably be able to break through it. Maybe even Kannis could.'

'And maybe not,' Manta snapped. 'We don't know – and that's the problem. What we really need now is *information* . . .'

I held up a hand, smiling faintly. A source of information had just arrived. April was back in my head.

'Nick, have you done something?' her inner voice cried. 'The castle's all in an uproar, watchmen rushing around, Kannis and Doul in a rage . . .'

'We had a little skirmish,' I told her in my mind, 'and now we're free and hiding. Hang on.'

Quickly I told Manta about the way April could

speak to me, and April confirmed that it'd be too risky to open another psychic connection to Manta or Bertrand. So as April and I talked, I stopped now and then to tell the others what I'd learned. It was clumsy, but it worked well enough.

She told me that when Doul reported that we hadn't arrived, the Head nearly blew the roof off in his fury. And again when they discovered that some unknown warrior – Stoll had only the vaguest memory of who'd hit her – had got us away.

But now a search of the castle was being organized, as I'd expected. April promised to warn us if any searchers got near our hideaway.

Along with all that, April was bubbling with excitement over Manta being there with all her power. And she was pleased that I'd managed, more or less, to get over all the hate and resentment I'd once felt for Manta.

I thought about telling April that Manta was her mother, but it seemed just about the worst time for that news. So I kept quiet, listening to April being happily still astounded that Manta had been Julia all along.

'It was a fantastic disguise,' she whispered. 'But – Julia was always so nice. I think I'm going to miss her.'

Manta smiled at that when I passed it on.

'But I guess she's still part of Manta,' April said, 'and I can't wait to get to know *her* better.'

No one bothered to add the three obvious extra words – 'if we live'.

As that lull went on, April told us a few useful things. The good news was that there were only the four sorcerers in the castle, and no servitors. The insect-watchmen did both jobs. But the bad news was that there were about fifty or so of them.

And since they were formed by Kannis's magic, he could make replacements. So no matter how many we killed or damaged, there'd always be more.

But the worst and weirdest stuff April told us concerned the Head. Stoll had told the truth that the giant Head was a form taken by an unnamed demon lord from a horror-realm. An ancient, ageless monstrosity who had begun invading our world in the distant past, to hunt and devour its favourite prey – humans.

When the demon first began his raids, back then, he came in his full form – an enormous, terrifying giant with a body to match the Head that we now saw, and with even more enormous magical powers. But in time some mighty tribal shamans gathered to fight him, combining their own powers – finally driving him back into his own realm.

And then they raised a mighty *barrier*, specially made so that his huge, dark magic was deflected by it, useless against it. So he was held back forever, penned in his own foul, lightless realm, never to return.

Never, that is, until another evil arose that almost matched his own.

That was an age later, in this modern world. When a number of great mages who had given themselves evil sorcery joined forces to swell their powers. And among their first acts, they set out to destroy the barrier. Its magic hadn't been formed against human powers – so they believed they could free the giant demon lord and make an ally of him.

But they didn't quite manage it. They were able to make only a small breach in the barrier – a tiny magical gap. Which somehow meant that the demon lord could only send his *spirit* through, back into this world.

The spirit wasn't quite as magically powerful as the intact demon would have been. But he was still stronger than all the Cartel sorcerers put together, and then some. With that power he made a magical copy of his own giant Head to contain himself in this world, and got back to his evil ways.

But this time he didn't simply start to feed on humans again. The world had changed, and had more than just food to offer.

So the disembodied demon within his artificial Head joined with the sorcerers – to form the Cartel.

It quickly became rich and powerful and ever more

evil. But though its sorcerers struggled tirelessly, they never managed to do any more damage to the barrier.

'It means the Head has one small weakness,' April said, 'which could help. You know about the little beings that are magically *made* for him, somewhere in the castle. They're alive in a weird way – and he eats their heads, feeding on their *life force*. But that's not enough for him. Fairly often he has to go back through the breach to his own realm. Back into his real body, to restore himself.'

Alderon had said something about that, I thought. So there were times when the monstrosity would be away, recharging his batteries.

Which would be a very good time for us to go and try to do what we came for.

'The trouble is,' April added, her mental voice sounding distressed, 'Kannis and the others think that they now have what the Head needs. That's why they're so desperate to catch me and do whatever they can to control me.'

'Because you're extra powerful,' I said.

'And because,' April said, 'there's a *prophecy*, from years and years ago—'

'We heard about that,' I broke in, and gave her a quick account of our visit to Alderon.

'Then you know it's about me,' she whispered. 'I'm

the Empowered Child they're waiting for. I'll have even more power, I think, when I'm older.'

'So you're supposed to make the Cartel invincible,' I said.

'In a special way, Nick.' She made a small sound like a mental sob. 'When I'm ready, the prophecy says – these are the exact words – I'll be the one whose magic *will make the Lord of the Cartel whole and entire at last*!'

33

I was a bit choked up myself when I relayed that to the others, who both looked appalled.

'That means bringing the barrier down,' Bertrand said, his voice shaky, 'so the demon won't have to send just his spirit through . . .'

'Is she quite sure?' Manta asked. 'That she's the one?'

When I asked April that, she said she'd heard Kannis and Doul talking about it, and *they* were definitely sure. Which was what mattered.

'Hang on,' Bertrand said. 'She's incredibly powerful as she is, and she'd be more so if she linked with Manta and me. So why don't we try now, instead, to *close* the breach?'

It seemed a great idea – for a moment.

'We'd be attacked by Kannis and Doul and Harmal while we tried,' April said sadly. 'And I don't want to be rude, but I don't think Bertrand and Manta would add enough power to let us hold all of them off and work on the breach at the same time.' She did the small sob again. 'Anyway, there's something else. It seems that those old shamans who set up the barrier in the first place paid a terrible price. The spell sort of burned them out, used up all their life force. They *died*, Nick. So did a few of the evil mages, later, from making just that one little breach.'

My spine turned cold. 'So if they're planning to force you to bring the whole barrier down, doing that could kill you?'

'Almost certainly,' she breathed. 'But I don't think they care. Getting their demon lord into this world, *all* of him, is all that matters to them.'

And when he's here, I thought, all in one piece, he'll be feasting on people again, and making the Cartel bigger and more evil, and maybe taking over the world . . .

'Then we'll definitely have to get you out of here,' I said. 'Any ideas?'

'Lots,' she said. 'Mostly about how impossible it seems. We have to stay free, even though they're searching everywhere. And my body has to be found, wherever they've hidden it, and brought close to me – so I can get back really fast, before their magic stops me.'

'Right,' I said.

'You'll need to find Paddy's and Sam's bodies too,' she said. 'And somehow get their bodies together with the two monsters that have their souls, then destroy the monsters.'

'Fine,' I said.

'And while you're doing all those things, you'll have to keep away from three powerful and desperate sorcerers and a small army of watchmen,' she went on. 'Kannis and Doul and Harmal will be using seeking spells, along with counter-spells to show any veiling magic you might use.'

'Piece of cake,' I said. 'As long as you stay in touch, give us what warnings and directions you can . . .'

She said nothing to that.

'April?' I said. 'You *will* be able to help us, won't you?'

Silence. Her inner voice had vanished from my mind.

Iciness touched my spine again as I told Manta and Bertrand. She went white; Bertrand sagged.

'You don't think . . .' he began. But then he saw my face and didn't say it.

And I didn't want to think it, but it was hard to stop. The fear that all the wild searching that was going on had finally discovered her hiding place.

'We have to move,' I said. 'If she needs help, we have to find her.'

But it wasn't April who needed help.

Her voice returned to my head, but my relief didn't last. It was nearly a shriek.

'Nick, you have to find somewhere else to hide!' she cried. 'Harmal and a squad of watchmen are close to you, looking *everywhere*!'

'We have to try to strengthen our veiling!' Bertrand urged, when I passed on the dire message.

'Against a Kannis counter-spell?' Manta said, looking dubious.

'No,' I said. 'If we hide here and the veiling doesn't work, we're trapped. We have to get moving. And *keep* moving, so they can't pin us down.'

It was a lesson I'd learned through years of being hunted, and I could see that Manta had learned it too. Bertrand moaned a little, but he wasn't about to stay in hiding by himself. So I drew the knife as we edged out of the pantry, found the corridor still empty and started running.

It wasn't a headlong sprint, since it wasn't a race and we didn't want to wear ourselves out. Anyway, speed alone wouldn't save us. We needed to be sneaky – and lucky.

But a moment later our luck ran out.

34

The corridor we were in brought us to a junction with another, wider corridor.

And around the corner, just as we reached it, came Harmal and a squad of six watchmen.

Everyone was startled – Harmal gasped and Bertrand yelped – but good old survival reflex did its job. I slashed with the knife to block a spear heading for Manta, then turned the slash into a swipe across Harmal's face.

As she screamed and reeled back I heard Bertrand scream as well, but I had no time to look. Though she was stumbling and bleeding, Harmal was still in the game, yelling a single spiky word.

Blue flame hissed from her hand, straight at my face. I was quick enough again to dodge, but I hadn't expected the second blast from her other hand that hit me like a fiery sledgehammer, high on my chest.

I crashed to the floor with a howl of pain, the charred wound gushing blood. I had a glimpse of

Bertrand also on the floor, blood pouring from a gash in his head and a leg wound. With three dead watchmen lying wasted around him. But the others were poising their spears, jaws gnashing, and Harmal was still standing . . .

Until Manta leaped like a kung-fu master and drove the toe of her boot into the woman's midriff with all her weight behind it.

Harmal's collapse seemed to shock the three remaining watchmen and, before they could move, Manta's book was in her hand again. Three large chunks of the ceiling crashed neatly down on the three armoured heads, and the watchmen collapsed. Only stunned, of course, since Manta couldn't take even their lives.

As she whirled towards Bertrand and me, I started struggling to my feet.

'I'm all right,' I groaned. 'Nothing fatal . . . Help Bertrand.'

She could see that my gory wound was already starting to close up and heal, so she did as I said. 'He's badly hurt,' she murmured. 'We have to hide somewhere again, so I can work on getting him better.'

'You take him,' I muttered, gritting my teeth. 'I'm done with hiding. If we're going to live through the next while, we need April. So I'm going to find her body and somehow get it to that painting.'

She stared at me, huge green eyes unreadable. But

she knew better than anyone that I was used to facing Cartel horrors on my own – and that I was a survivor.

Her mouth moved in a small sad smile. 'Good luck,' she breathed.

Then she and Bertrand disappeared, or turned invisible, or whatever it was she did.

And I whispered, 'See you,' to the empty air and turned away.

Something like half an hour later – when I felt as if I would've aged several years if I could age at all – I was in another empty dim carpeted corridor. Getting nowhere.

How do you search an enormous castle that's full of criss-crossing corridors and stairways, siderooms and back rooms and ante-rooms, niches and alcoves, maybe secret passages for all I knew? All I could do was wander along, aimlessly, seeing what I could see. Hoping for a clue or a signpost or something.

Staying alert for all the deadly enemies who were searching for me.

I'd had one or two near misses – almost walking into a squad of watchmen coming out of a doorway, then running for cover while Doul stalked past with another squad of the insect men. And I had no idea how Doul's seeker magic hadn't spotted me.

Maybe Manta did something, wherever she was. Or

maybe, in the usual smug Cartel way, Doul wasn't bothering to be too careful and alert. But I was fairly sure that it hadn't been April who'd helped.

I hadn't had a word from her since I started out.

And what I really needed now was that awesome psychic gift of hers – to spot danger coming and to point me in the right direction.

In fact, though, it still wasn't clear to me how much of her magic she still had, in her disembodied form. Even the demon lord's super-powered spirit, in the Head, had to keep going back to its real body to restore itself.

Maybe April's spirit was getting *weaker*.

Which made it all the more desperately urgent to get her and her body together.

'April,' I whispered, aloud, as I crept along that corridor, 'if you can hear me – hang on. I'm on my way . . .'

Then I jumped as the air grew hazy in front of me – and Manta's face appeared in the haze.

'In fact, dear Nick,' her image said, 'you're on the *wrong* way.'

'What do you mean?' I gasped. 'Where are you? How's Bertrand? How are you *doing* this?'

'I've sent you messages like this before,' she said. 'Though you were usually sleeping then, so they were like dreams. Bertrand is healing, and so far we're safe.

But you've moved in a circle, so you're almost back to where you started.'

I groaned. 'Which way should I go?'

'That I can't tell you,' Manta said. 'My psychic power can reach to your mind, but it can't go looking around a building that I don't know. Nor can Bertrand's.'

'Mine can,' said another voice, joining the conversation.

April, in my head again. I almost shouted with relief.

'Nick, tell Manta to be quiet,' she went on quickly. 'Her psychic voice could be overheard. And tell her to stay where she is, with Bertrand.'

Manta gasped, and her inner voice went silent as her image vanished.

'April, are you all right?' I asked.

'I'm scared and lonely and feeling worn out,' she murmured, 'but I suppose you are too. I've been quiet because the Head linked with Kannis for a while to look for me. But now they've been distracted – some more trouble reported from the west country. I think they might send Harmal to deal with it . . .'

'I wish they'd send Kannis,' I muttered. 'Any chance you can help me? Manta said I was going the wrong way.'

'You're actually in a good place,' April said. 'I heard Kannis telling Doul that they'd have to put a guard on the stairs up to the west tower. I think that Kannis's private apartment is in the east tower, so there must be something else needing special protection in the west one . . .'

'Something like *you*,' I whispered. 'Your body.'

'Maybe,' she said. 'Anyway, you're just two corridors from the stairs up to that tower. If you can find a way past the guard they've set . . .'

'I'll find one,' I growled. 'If I have to, I'll find a way *through* them.'

It was a joy to have her in my mind again as I set off. Moments later I was easing open a heavy door and peering up a stairway. Not more back stairs for non-existent servants – these were wide steps of dark rich wood, gleaming with polish.

Bad news. Wooden steps often creak, just when you don't want them to. And the stairs were brightly lit, by lamps or perhaps a skylight at the top.

And I could hear the faint scrape of movement, high above me, and a *clink* that sounded a lot like a metal spearhead touching a wall. Above all, I could smell them – the rank acid stink of their insect bodies.

As I drew silently back, April's voice spoke again, sounding anxious. 'Nick, you can't fight them on that stairway . . .'

I'd already worked that out. Tackling a number of

spears stabbing down from above me was a really poor idea.

I'd had a better idea even before I opened the door.

Just a few steps away along the passage I'd seen a window. Looking out on to a grey and choppy sea. If I got out through that window, I'd be on an outer wall.

I climbed Doul's house, I thought grimly. Now I'll climb Kannis's castle.

35

The window was made of many squares of thick glass held together by a sort of lattice of metal strips. I couldn't find a latch, so it probably wasn't made to be opened. But it was all quite old and crusty, and the strips turned out to be surprisingly soft metal, perhaps lead. So the knife and I went to work.

It wasn't fun, fiddling with panes of glass while knowing that a Kannis seeker spell could spot me at any moment. But it didn't take too long to prise enough glass out and pull enough metal aside to let me squeeze through on to the outer sill.

I was pleased that I was out in daylight, able to see where I was going. I was also glad to see that the stones of the castle wall were very ancient and rugged, which I thought just about anyone could climb.

Best of all, the spell that kept the castle invisible acted like a sort of protective field around it. There was a stiff sea breeze, and spits of rain from low scudding clouds, but none of it reached the wall or me.

Still, the climb wasn't that easy. Despite all the stone's useful lumps and bulges and cracks, I was still clinging with only fingertips and toes, and that gets tiring. More so when I had to pause sometimes to chip mortar away with the knife when there wasn't a ready-made finger-hold. Above all, the tower was a *lot* higher than Doul's house had been.

I was also wound up tight with tension – not the best state for a demanding climb. But as I went on and up, no voices shouted their discovery, no demons or mages appeared to drag me down. It seemed that the searchers hadn't bothered to aim their seeking at the *outside* of the castle.

That helped to give me the nerve, when I reached a higher window, to move across and peer warily inside. It showed a rather lush bedroom, all dark wood and rich furnishings with a huge deep bed. And I could see part of an even more lush lounge through the bedroom door.

April had said that Kannis had his private apartment in the other tower, so I wondered if this one might be Doul's.

But I didn't really care. What mattered was that it was empty, so no one would be crashing through the window to attack me.

Even so, I went on being tense, half expecting to be spotted. And also worrying about April and Manta and all of them. I tried to block those thoughts, to focus on the climb, but they kept creeping in and unsettling me.

So did the fact that my fingertips were getting scraped raw on the stone. I knew things would get really dodgy if they started bleeding. Blood is slippery.

Before long, I jammed the knife deep into a crevice between blocks of stone and just hung there, until my tiredness faded and the damage to my fingers healed.

I was high above the island by then, as glad as I'd ever been that the knife was unbreakable. And when I looked up I was more glad to see that I'd got fairly close to the top – with the narrow slit of another window not far above.

I climbed on, forcing myself not to hurry. It'd be really stupid to make a slip after coming that far. So I was extra concentrated and careful as I struggled up beside the narrow window and edged sideways a little to take a look.

I was more or less praying that I could get through that window somehow. I badly didn't want to have to climb all the way back down. It's definitely no fun at all to go that way on an almost sheer surface.

But most of all I was praying that, after all my efforts, April's soulless body really would be there.

And it was.

My heart leaped in my chest as I saw her sitting quietly in a chair, completely still, empty-eyed as ever.

I also saw that the window was on hinges, and used the knife as a lever to get it open before swinging it wide.

She watched me calmly, as if the sight of someone climbing through the highest window in the castle was perfectly normal. 'Hello, Nick,' she said, her voice as blank as her face.

'I've come to take you out of here,' I said, panting a little as I enjoyed the feeling of my feet solidly on dark, firm wooden floorboards.

But I was still tense. I remembered that she was totally obedient, but I feared that Kannis might have commanded her *not* to obey anyone else's commands.

'All right,' she said. 'But the door is locked from the outside.'

It was a relief that she would obey me. But the possibility of a locked door hadn't really occurred to me. I'd been too concentrated on just getting to her.

Now I had to find a way past the lock, and then somehow manage to take her past the watchmen guarding the stairs below.

For a moment I had a wild idea of trying to climb back down the outside wall with April clinging to my back. Not possible. Though she wasn't all that heavy, I'd need to be Spider-Man for that trick.

And, I found, I'd need to be Superman to get through the heavy door's thick dark wood, tightly fitted, with a big metal keyhole and no key.

I thought of using the knife to chop away the wood around the hinges. But the wood had hardened during the long life of the castle, and I reckoned it would take hours to get through it. And then the big hinges might be immovable . . .

So I stood there feeling hopeless, trying to think, with April behind me waiting patiently to be told what to do.

And a key suddenly rattled in the lock, and the door was flung open.

Two insect watchmen charged in, lunging at me with their spears.

36

I tried to spin away, but collided with April. She was flung back towards her chair as I fell to one side, off balance.

And the watchmen cackled with glee, and struck.

I managed to dodge one stabbing spear and chopped at the other with the knife. So its long spearhead – edges sharpened like a sword-blade – stabbed into my thigh, not my chest. As blood spurted from that wound, the first watchman swung his spear like an axe at my neck. I jerked away, but not far enough, and the blade bit deep into my upper arm.

The impact also knocked me off my feet. Dazed with pain, bleeding all over the place, I sprawled helplessly on the floor while the two monsters cackled and cawed with savage glee and raised their spears again.

But blood is even more slippery on polished wood. The first watchman came at me too eagerly, and slipped, tumbling beside me.

I might have been half stunned, but my survivor

autopilot wasn't. The knife slashed through his neck almost as he hit the floor. Then I rolled, ignoring the agony of my wounds, grabbed the dead one's spear and stabbed upward just as the second one stabbed down.

I got there first, just barely, so he missed. His corpse fell into the growing pool of my blood and twitched momentarily as the life drained out of it.

And as I staggered to my feet, the door stood wide open.

So were the big hazel eyes of April's body as she watched me bleed. The wound in my thigh might have nicked an artery, since the blood was jetting halfway across the room. But I wound my belt around my leg above the gash, pulled it agonizingly tight, gasped, 'Come on,' and headed out.

As I stumbled down the stairs, with April following, I started to shiver – from the blood loss. But I tried to ignore it. I'd mostly stopped the bleeding from the serious leg wound, so the usual healing process would have a chance. Both wounds were already closing a little.

Anyway, that was no time to start being weak and shaky. I had to get April's body to the portrait of the old witch before anyone else came to kill me.

But we'd only crept some way down, and my shakiness had got slightly better, when I heard the pounding of heavy feet on the stairs below.

It could have been worse. I wasn't bleeding much

any more, so I wasn't leaving a trail. And we'd just passed another heavy wooden door, with some elegant carving on its panels, which had to lead into the lush apartment that was probably Doul's.

And when I lurched back up the few steps with April, I found that Mr Doul didn't bother to lock his door – since, of course, who would *dare* to invade his private space?

I would. And we did, whisking inside and closing the door. No key to lock it with – but beyond the small entrance hall there was the huge luxurious living room, full of large furniture and nooks and crannies, and doors to other rooms.

So we hid, with me desperately hoping that whoever was coming up would go on past to check on the prisoner at the top.

It was a fairly faint hope of course, with top-level sorcerers doing seeker spells. And the hope didn't last long.

The panelled outer door crashed open. But this time it wasn't insect watchmen with skinny, sliceable necks who came storming in.

It was the two huge crystal monsters with Sam's and Paddy's faces.

And Harmal behind them, wild eyes ablaze with fury.

*

In a way, it was her very fury that saved me. She was probably on her way to being a little unhinged, like Fray – and of course she wasn't afraid of me, confident in her power. Maybe she had an urge to taste my blood, like Gavaric. Maybe, even then, they still wanted to take me alive.

I didn't know, didn't ask, didn't care.

All I knew was that her magic could have bound me or blasted me from across the room, but she didn't use it.

Instead she pushed the two monsters aside and leaped at me.

As she leaped her neck stretched out and her green-veined face grew lumpy and lizard-like, with long multi-fanged jaws.

I half dodged, slamming my right hand up under the jaws to push the fangs away. As she hissed in rage, her hand, now thick-skinned with long claws, slashed at my arm, and the jaws opened wide again.

But I growled, 'Look what I found.' And I drove the golden blade of the knife hilt-deep into the green scaliness of her throat.

Her blood was greenish too, as it burst out like a fountain. I reeled round, ready to stab again, only to see her visibly weakening, trying to claw and snap at me as she sank to the floor – dead.

And then the crystal monsters charged at me.

But weirdly, as they moved, the one with Sam's face seemed to lurch sideways, blundering into the other one. Obviously Harmal's control of them had slipped away with her life. As they stumbled, I tried to leap past them to the door, pulling April with me. But for all their size they recovered quickly, and one of them grabbed me and dragged me back.

April crept away, watching blankly as I found my balance and struck at that one with the knife. But it just glanced off the shiny surface. And the monster, the one like Paddy, swung a massive fist.

It hit me on the side of the face and I felt my jaw shatter. Stunned, I was flung to the floor, where the other one delivered a brutal kick that smashed a few ribs. I shrieked, half blind with pain, unable to do anything but curl myself up as they loomed over me, side by side, and took turns kicking me.

I felt a kneecap give way – another kick opened my leg wound again, adding my blood to Harmal's on the floor. Without her to control them, they seemed to be on autopilot, trying to kill me no matter what. They obviously hadn't quite got the 'try to take him alive' bit.

Another giant crystal foot slammed into my side. I could feel myself almost longing for the dark embrace that would take away my pain when I blearily saw movement behind them.

It was Manta, all fiery green eyes and red-gold hair

streaming behind her like tongues of flame, leaping at the two hulking shiny bodies.

She swung an arm up and around each of their thick necks and jerked backwards.

The unexpected attack caught them off guard, so that they lurched back a step or two away from me.

A second more and they would have broken free and turned to deal with the intruder who was interrupting their fun kickabout.

But they didn't get that second.

Manta stared past them, her eyes drilling into mine. '*Save her*!' she screamed.

In the same instant, with a sound like an exploding grenade, a jagged hole appeared in the floor where they were standing.

And all three plunged down through that opening, out of sight.

37

Silently screaming myself, in agony, I slowly dragged my broken, bleeding self to the edge of the hole and looked down. I expected to see Manta and the monsters lying hurt, or worse, on whatever floor it was that lay below. But I didn't.

I saw another floor with a jagged hole in it – and yet another hole in the floor far below that. With only darkness to be seen in those depths.

Manta had made sure it would be a *long* fall.

Maybe it would have been long enough to kill the monsters. Which would mean that Paddy's and Sam's souls would be freed. But with nowhere to go.

It would also mean that if Manta somehow survived the fall, she would have lost her powers – because she had taken lives.

Or maybe the fall had simply killed her too.

These thoughts trailed dimly through my mind, which was mostly occupied with fighting my pain and trying not to slide into unconsciousness. I couldn't let that happen. Manta had told me, though I didn't need telling, to save April.

The trouble was that I couldn't work out how to save myself.

I was seriously damaged in too many places. I didn't think any of it was fatal – I'd clamped a hand over the leg wound to shut the bleeding down. But it was going to take longer than usual for all those injuries to be restored. I could barely find a part of me that hadn't sustained any damage. Yet I knew that time was a luxury I didn't have.

For those moments the stairs down were clear, but that wouldn't last. Very soon somebody else would be along – Doul or Kannis and a mob of insect-watchmen.

I'd just run out of choices.

'Come here,' I croaked.

April's soulless body obediently stepped towards me, neatly avoiding the pool of blood.

'Do you know how to find the portrait of the old witch-woman with a blue face?' I asked.

'Yes,' she said.

'I want you to go there,' I gasped.

'If you wish,' she said.

'And go really quickly,' I told her. 'Fast as you can. But if someone comes along, hide. Don't let *anyone* see you. Understand?'

'Yes,' she said. And she turned and ran towards the door.

That's the best I can do, April, I thought. But though I held my breath and listened hard, there was no reply.

I exhaled slowly and focused on my broken body, piece by piece fixing itself, as a wave of exhaustion rippled over me and my eyes closed into the abyss of unconsciousness.

I came to to the sound of footsteps clamouring on the stairs and sharp echoing voices. I did a quick mental scan of my body – back to normal, fourteen forever, changeless – and for once I felt quite grateful for it. I glanced quickly round the room. There was only one door so I'd have to leave the way I came in – something I really didn't fancy doing with half the Cartel and their dreadful minions charging up the stairs towards me. I'd taken enough of a battering today to last me a lifetime.

I turned to the gaping hole in the floor where Manta and the two stone demons had plunged away into nothingness. I wasn't too keen on joining them. It was a long way down, and if the impact was swift enough and brutal enough it would kill me.

The voices came closer and I made my decision. I turned my back to the hole and jumped backwards into its gaping maw. But before I fell too far I swung my hands forward and grabbed on to the jagged ledge, my body jerking to a halt as I gripped the splintered wood for all I was worth. I heard someone – something – enter the room. It wouldn't take too long for them to notice the fingers poking over the edge of the hole. I swung myself silently, aiming for the floor below. One final swing and I lurched forward with my feet, my hands ripping on the ledge as I fell towards the ground. The impact was intense and I felt my ankle explode in pain.

Stoll's ugly little head appeared over the ledge. 'At last I've found you,' she said in a voice filled with excitement. 'My masters will be pleased.'

'You've found me,' I sneered, 'but you haven't got me.' I limped again to the edge of the hole, and repeated the same trick I'd used on the floor above. But just as I released my grip and swung through the air towards the floor below, Stoll leaped over the edge towards me. And as she did so her arms stretched out and leathery flaps grew from her body to meet her now long, claw-like hands, as her face twisted into a velvety bat-like snout and she swooped down and plucked me out of the air, with the talons that had replaced her feet, like a vole in a field of corn. She shrieked with delight as her claws punctured my flesh.

I unsheathed my knife and slashed wildly towards her, but her grip was such that I couldn't twist round and my arm couldn't extend far enough behind me to make contact. All I could do was to wait for her to make her landing and release me from her grip, and hope that it wasn't in the middle of even more maniacs baying for my blood.

38

So much for hope. Stoll let out a blood-curdling screech and flapped her wings hard, rising up through the hole in the floor above and dropping me at the feet of two waiting watchmen, as a furious Doul marched into the room. I slipped my knife quickly away, sensing this was not the time to pick a fight with a high-powered high-level Cartel mage. Especially as I had no back-up.

'Take him to the Head,' he raged. 'NOW!'

I decided to act like the compliant prisoner for now and watch for a better chance of escape or attack. So I let the guards march me meekly back to the same wood-panelled room where I'd seen the Head before, and when I got there I didn't know whether to laugh or cry . . . They had April.

She stood there docile and blank-eyed, just as she had been when I'd sent her on her way to find her soul.

I cursed inwardly, hope seeping from me. She can't have got there.

But then I heard her in my mind. I kept my head down and stifled my reactions.

'Nick,' she said, 'it's me. I'm in my body. But they don't know it. I need to keep quiet. Look up if you've heard me.'

I raised my head and looked up to the vast vaulted ceiling towering in the distance above me. I didn't dare look over at April in case I was spotted and gave the game away. But fortunately for me, April and I were able to exchange a brief glance as a suitable distraction was found in the form of Bertrand being dragged noisily into the room.

'Unhand me!' he shouted. 'This really is too much!'

He took in the scene around him and flinched at seeing April – his daughter – docile and vacant, apparently still in the thrall of the Cartel.

'How sweet,' Doul spat through his hideous black lips. 'The three of you back together. Such a shame it can't be for long.' He laughed hysterically but stopped as the heavy curtain above the raised area swished open and the terrifying Head loomed into view.

'Enough!' he shouted, his voice volcanic in strength. 'There has been enough time wasted on these pathetic specimens. I will waste no more. We have the girl. We will find her soul and she will do our bidding. Mark my words – it is written in the prophecy. She will do our bidding. You are merely a trifling irritation. You and that meddling wizard of the west.'

Alderon! Surely that was who he meant. What had the old man been up to?

'He thought to destroy us, working through our cells one by one. But instead we have destroyed him. Kannis has finally put an end to his nonsense.'

A sudden burst of rage swept through me and I thrust against the watchmen who held me, causing them to tighten their pincer grip on me. I groaned with the pain.

The Head laughed. 'Always so brave, Changeless One. I wonder if you will be so brave when you finally make the only change that ever really matters. The change from life to death.' He flicked his eyes to the right and a large door swung open.

Now I know I haven't had much schooling, but I've seen plenty of pictures and read plenty of books and I know what a man in a black mask holding a large axe is planning.

There was going to be an execution, and with a grim dread I realized that it was going to be my head on the block.

I looked desperately at Bertrand. All the colour had drained from his face and he looked like he was going to faint. The Cartel had finally cottoned on. If it was swift enough and brutal enough, it would kill me. Even I couldn't recover from being decapitated.

A coldness like I had never felt before washed over me. It was as if my veins ran with icy water.

Two watchmen came in carrying a heavy wooden block in front of them. It had a round indentation in the surface of it, just perfect for resting a neck and head on. Bertrand and April remained frozen as I was dragged, protesting, over to the block.

So many times I'd imagined my death. Slashed in a desperate fight against some unspeakable evil creature, crushed or smashed or sliced in the heat of some terrifying battle. But no scenario I'd come up with was as gut-wrenchingly bad as this. The cold, calm steel of the axeman's blade.

I was pushed to my knees in front of the block, I felt the cool smooth surface of the wood on my cheek. I held my breath. The world stopped. As the executioner picked up his axe and swung it ferociously above his head.

39

The next moment, all hell seemed to break loose around me. Bertrand had obviously tried to muster some magic to help me and had sent the axe flying backwards out of the executioner's hands to land embedded in the wood of the wall behind him. Doul had instantly sent a flaming blue arc straight at Bertrand's chest and he sank, in agony, to his knees. In the confusion the ant-watchmen momentarily lessened their grip on me and I managed to break free and, knife in hand, slashed at both their puny necks in one rounding motion.

Doul then fixed his eyes on me and, pointing two fingers in my direction, he muttered something under his breath. I felt a weight like an avalanche pressing down on me. I sank down to the ground, unable to stand against the force. It was as if gravity had just increased tenfold and all the weight of the universe was focused on one point – me. I lay crushed on the floor, desperate for air but unable to breathe, my lungs squashed down to nothing, my chest unable to rise. I could feel the pressure behind my eyes, I felt like my head was going to explode and I knew for sure there was no way I could recover from such a death. If they kept the pressure on me, my time to regenerate would elapse. I was going to die.

I looked longingly over to April. I couldn't bear the thought of never seeing her again and of leaving her in these circumstances, completely unprotected. Maybe the prophecy would play out after all and there was nothing I could do about it.

But as I looked into April's eyes I could see she wasn't going to let that happen. She raised her hands and screamed, and as she did so Doul flew up into the air and was smashed against the wall at the far end of the hall.

I felt the pressure lift from me in an instant. Air rushed into my lungs with such force that I felt unable to control my breathing and gasped in great gulps of it. I staggered to my feet as April fought off all comers. Watchmen were flying around the room, Doul was lying crumpled and broken in a corner. Bertrand cowered, still in the grip of his captors. I ran over at full pelt and leaped, feet first, towards the first watchman holding him. Stoll, back in her normal pudgy form, was running over towards us, just beginning to unveil her ugly talons and shark-like fangs. She rose off the ground, her great wings unfurling, just as I arced towards her with the knife and slashed an immense slit down the middle of her belly, feeling the soft wet contents wash over my arm as she plummeted to the ground.

Suddenly the great door at the end of the room opened again and Kannis rushed in. He took one look at the scene before him and raised his hands in a terrifying gesture of power, sweeping over the whole room as the Head spoke again. 'Hold them, Kannis. But don't harm the girl. She is complete.'

The scene froze as we were all held in a tableau of violence.

'Now,' the Head thundered, 'you will do my bidding.'

His giant eyes turned to fire in his head and shot two laser-like lines out towards April. She seemed to be consumed in their glow. Engulfed in flames and yet seemingly unharmed. Her eyes lit up like amber.

'You will do my bidding,' the Head repeated. 'We have waited for this moment. The time is now right. Open the rift, join our worlds, rejoice in my power!'

I watched in horror as April seemed to struggle and writhe in the Head's forceful grip. At first she shot out sparks and jerked violently as she tried to fight against him, but as the battle of wills went on she seemed to weaken until she seemed like no more than a puppet on a string, controlled by him as he tugged at her senses.

I could see Doul gathering himself by the far wall, dusting down his pristine white suit, his eyes aglow at what he was witnessing. Kannis too seemed to bathe in the heat of the Head's demonic powers, soaking in the scene while never letting go of the grip he had over Bertrand and myself.

I looked at Bertrand, who seemed as horror-struck as I was. Was this what it had come to? That we would watch April being forced to capitulate? Surely even she wouldn't be able to fight against the Head? For a brief moment I thought that I would rather be dead.

And then, as I saw April raise her hands, her face now blank and stony again, I truly did wish I had died and didn't have to witness what was to happen next.

The Head opened his cavernous mouth and a laugh like the hounds of hell erupted from him as a huge chasm began ripping up through the wall of the castle behind him. The whole place shook and pictures and hangings began to rattle loose from the walls.

April's eyes had completely rolled back in her head and a strange babbling language was pouring out from her mouth.

'Yes!' the Head roared. 'Yes, my child! Make me complete!'

And as he said it, it was as if the world was ripped

in two, like a black hole imploding into an endless night.

And then I saw Manta.

40

Doul and Kannis saw her at the same time. The shock made Kannis momentarily relax his grip, and Bertrand and I both saw our chance and lunged, one each, towards the mages. Bertrand managed some quick restraining spell on Doul while I went straight for brute force and stabbed Kannis deep in the neck.

He shrieked in pain and wheeled round, arms raised, about to wreak some terrible revenge on me, but he hadn't banked on Manta. I had never seen her this way. She was enraged. Angrier than I had ever seen anyone before. She forced him to his knees and held him there while snake-like vines bound themselves tightly around him. Unable to kill him, she had to incapacitate him. Leave the killing to me, I thought bitterly. She flicked her hand and Kannis went limp, his head lolling to one side, his flabby tongue drooping from his slavering mouth.

I turned my attention to Bertrand, who was involved in a battle of wills with Doul. And it seemed Doul was getting the upper hand. Bertrand was on his knees, his hands at his throat as if he was being strangled. He was struggling for breath, his eyes bulging in his skull. I ran towards him, but Doul, with a flick of a wrist, knocked me off my feet. I was winded but unhurt. I lay for a second awaiting my moment, playing dead. Doul turned momentarily to check the Head's progress, and I pounced. I landed on his back and clung on like a monkey. I forced my knife under his chin, the blade perfectly placed against the front of his neck. Then, with all the force I could muster, I pulled across and back and felt the sinews and flesh ripping under the razor-sharp edge of my knife. I felt Doul's warm blood spurt across my hand as his body went limp beneath me.

The few remaining watchmen seemed not to know what to do. With Doul dead and Kannis incapacitated it seemed no one was controlling them. They ran around snapping at each other – antennae and limbs dropping like rain and breaking with a sickening crunch underfoot.

I turned to Manta.

'April!' she screamed. 'April, you are my daughter. I am your mother. I love you. I have always loved you. You must come back to me!'

The Head laughed as the sky opened up around us. Gusts of wind were blowing through the great hall.

Manta's hair streamed out around her. It seemed she had not broken through.

'April,' she screamed again, 'come back to me!'

And slowly April's head turned towards her mother, and a soft light of recognition came into her eyes.

Manta beckoned to Bertrand. 'Join with me,' she shouted over the roar of the night.

Manta and Bertrand joined hands and looked together towards April. 'Our child,' they shouted, 'come back to us!'

And a switch seemed to flick somewhere inside April's mind as she looked towards her parents.

An arc of light shot from them to her, not like the intense fire of the Head, but a soft, soothing light, the most perfect hue of delicate rose.

'NO!' the Head roared. 'You will not have her!'

But Manta, Bertrand and April all raised their hands together and the power surge was incredible. And the amazing thing was, you could tell it was a force for good and not for evil, though it was still terrifyingly strong.

'No!' the Head roared again. But this time there was an edge of pain in the voice and the creeping note of panic.

Manta let go of Bertrand and spun around. 'Focus through me, my darling,' she called to April. 'Together we can defeat them.'

And the two of them locked in the most intense and loving gaze I have ever seen.

Then things got seriously scary. The building was falling apart around us – bits of masonry flying, flashes like lightning erupting all over the place. The noise was deafening.

The Head was swelling and shrinking like a wave in a storm. Screaming and writhing, spitting out flames and spurting acid liquid. It was all I could do to stay standing.

And then everything collapsed around us. I was running, dodging falling masonry. I saw something large and heavy falling towards Kannis, but I never stopped to see if it landed on target. I was trying to get to Manta and Bertrand and April, who were now grouped together in a tight little huddle, their forces combined to crush the mighty Head.

And with one final emotional charge they succeeded and the world exploded before me as years of evil and corruption spewed out into nothing in a sulphuric volcano of rage and hate.

There was stuff flying everywhere; images of past terrors rose up and faded away with equal speed. The Head was dying, and in his death throes his hideous, vast lifetime of cruelty spun around him before fading to nothing.

I stood transfixed. So much so that I didn't notice a

large bit of rock hurtling around the bend towards me. It crashed into the side of my face, and in a searing arc of pain I descended into darkness.

41

I woke up with the most almighty headache of my life. At least the most almighty headache I'd had since becoming permanently fourteen. Usually by the time I came to, things were starting to straighten themselves out. So this was weird.

Perhaps I hadn't been out for as long as I thought. I looked around me. I was lying on the island. And it was just that again. A sandy plateau with a few tufts of marram grass on it. A wave of joy washed over me. We'd done it, we'd beaten the Cartel.

I rolled over on to one elbow and propped myself up. I could hear voices. I squinted into the distance. I could see Manta and April and Bertrand all huddled around something.

I got carefully to my feet. I couldn't believe how much my head still hurt as I limped gingerly over to them.

When I looked down I felt sick.

The three were crouched round the lifeless bodies of

Sam and Paddy. Manta was crying. April was holding some strange spherical object in her hand and muttering an incantation.

'What's going on?' I hissed at Bertrand.

'It's over,' Bertrand said. 'We defeated the Cartel but . . .' he gestured at the bodies of the two men, 'it seems we've paid a heavy price.'

'What's April doing?' I asked, aghast. I couldn't cope with the thought of losing Sam and Paddy, two of the only people in the world who'd ever given a stuff about me.

'It's their souls,' Bertrand said. 'In that sphere. Manta managed to unlock them from those stone creatures when she threw herself down that hole. She kept them safe in the sphere. But their bodies . . . well, we're not sure we've got to them in time . . .'

We stood silently as April finished her incantation and opened the sphere. Two wisps of silvery air seemed to swirl momentarily in front of us.

We held our breaths.

The wispy swirls circled round the two men, then entered their bodies through their mouths.

Nothing.

Manta gulped back a sob. 'Oh Paddy,' she cried touching his hand. 'Please, Paddy, no . . .'

She sank into April's arms – bereft.

And then, a gasp from Paddy and a gasp from Sam

and the two men stirred from where they lay. Looking around, at first baffled and then smiling. And we were all shrieking and dancing and crying and hugging each other like crazy. April had done it.

But then a thought occurred to me. Manta had *removed* their souls, so why hadn't *she* put them back?

April looked at me and smiled, knowing what I was thinking. 'Manta isn't magical any more, Nick,' she said.

I blinked in astonishment.

'She took life – the Head, Kannis, several watchmen. She broke her covenant.'

I rubbed my head again. It still really hurt.

April reached out and took my hand. 'And there was another of her acts that was reversed if she broke her covenant . . .'

I looked at her questioningly, still rubbing my sore head. My hand stopped midway through. My head still hurt. It hadn't changed back!

'You're no longer changeless, Nick,' she said, grinning. 'It's over . . . It's all over.'

I sank to my knees, suddenly too weak to stand.

I wasn't changeless any more. I wasn't stuck at fourteen forever.

I could live out my life, however long or short it might be. I could grow old with April by my side.

Manta was right: she had done me a favour – I wasn't

just some homeless kid, dead in a gutter. I was part of a family. And I had my whole life ahead of me. And for the first time in my whole life, I could look forward without fear . . .

Douglas Hill

One day at a time . . .

One demon at a time . . .

Nick Walker has been fourteen for years. Branded with the Mark of Changelessness, he will never age. And he is virtually indestructible – broken bones and torn flesh heal almost instantly.

But now a deadly challenge lies ahead. The Cartel's most powerful demons are roaming the country, lusting for Nick's blood. With only a knife for protection, it's kill or be killed . . .

The first horrifying instalment in the DEMON STALKERS trilogy.

DEMON STALKERS

TORMENT

Douglas Hill

Bring it on, I yelled silently while the wraiths howled . . .

Nick Walker has been branded with the Mark of Changelessness – he will never age and his wounds heal instantly. But that won't stop the Cartel's evil demons from doing their best to destroy him.

Now on a quest to rescue his friends, Nick finds himself in a hell-like netherworld. Here he must battle his old demons again . . . only this time they're *already dead.*

The second horrifying instalment in the DEMON STALKERS trilogy.

CHANGELING

STEVE FEASEY

Is he a boy or is he a beast?

Trey thinks he is an ordinary teenager. Then he meets Lucien Charron – a mysterious stranger with eyes that seem flecked with fire and skin that blisters in sunlight. Suddenly Trey finds himself living in a luxury penthouse at the heart of a strange and sinister empire built on the powers of the Netherworld – vampires, demons, sorcerers, djinn. And Trey discovers his own secret: a power that's roaring to break free.

Meet the last hereditary werewolf. One thing's for sure: Trey Laporte will never be ordinary again.